How much had she forgotten?

As Sergeant Troy Stoner smiled at her, her pulse fluttered in her throat. He really was quite attractive, Andrea thought, and wondered why she hadn't noticed when he'd questioned her last night.

Maybe she had noticed. Maybe she'd forgotten. She'd forgotten her own husband, she thought, guiltily fingering her wedding ring.

She looked away, unable to hold Sergeant Stoner's probing gaze. "Have you remembered anything?"

"My name." She was still unable to meet his gaze. "It's Andrea."

"So I heard. It's very pretty. And your last name?"

"I don't know." With an effort, Andrea willed herself to relax, forced her gaze to meet Sergeant Stoner's. His eyes, a dark impenetrable brown, were fringed with long, curly lashes. He was tall and lean, but Andrea knew that beneath his suit coat, the muscles in his arms and chest would be powerful. She could almost feel them flex and bunch beneath her hands.

She stopped her thoughts cold. Was she remembering how it felt to be in a man's arms? Or was she experiencing wishful thinking, because of this *particular* man?

Just what kind of a woman am I?

Books by Amanda Stevens

HARLEQUIN INTRIGUE
373—STRANGER IN PARADISE
388—A BABY'S CRY
397—A MAN OF SECRETS

The Second Mrs. Malone
Amanda Stevens

Harlequin Books

TORONTO • NEW YORK • LONDON
AMSTERDAM • PARIS • SYDNEY • HAMBURG
STOCKHOLM • ATHENS • TOKYO • MILAN
MADRID • WARSAW • BUDAPEST • AUCKLAND

This book is lovingly dedicated to Steven, Lucas and Leanne Amann

ISBN 0-373-22430-3

THE SECOND MRS. MALONE

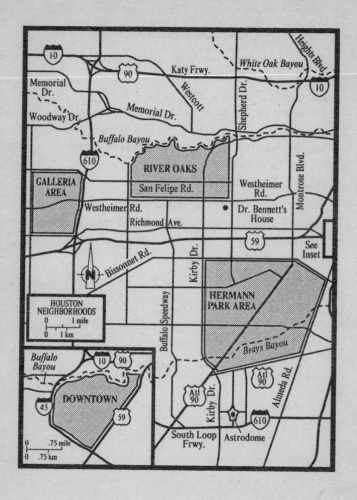

CAST OF CHARACTERS

Andrea Malone—What secrets does she harbor?

Sergeant Troy Stoner—Is he falling for an innocent victim or a cold-blooded murderess?

Dr. Claudia Bennett—Can she unlock the secrets hidden in the deepest recesses of Andrea's mind?

Paul Bellamy—The dead man's partner.

Robert Malone—The dead man's brother.

Dorian Andropolous—The dead man's former mother-in-law.

Richard Malone—The dead man.

Chapter One

The woman was covered in blood. The drying crimson splashed across the front of her expensive white tank dress like globs of red paint. Her pale face was streaked with dirt and mascara, and her blond hair hung to her waist in damp, matted clumps. She looked as if she'd been to hell and back, and Sergeant Troy Stoner of the Houston Police Department couldn't take his eyes off her.

He turned to the patrol officer who had picked her up earlier in the evening after spotting her wandering down a busy street and brought her to the emergency room at St. Mary's.

"Who is she?" Troy asked over the noise and chaos of the ER. Thunder boomed outside, and somewhere down the hallway, a baby cried incessantly while a man with a gunshot wound in his leg screamed obscenities in Spanish at one of the nurses.

Officer Dermott shrugged his damp shoulders, oblivious to the general confusion around him. "Hell if I know. I couldn't find any identification on her, and she was pretty disoriented when I picked her up. Didn't say one word the whole way here." He paused and tapped his left temple with his fingertip. "I figure they'll take her up to the bin after they check her out here."

Troy frowned at the derogatory term for the psychiatric ward, although to be honest, he couldn't say it had ever bothered him before. But something about this woman brought out something in him he didn't care to analyze. Unable to tear his gaze away, he stared at her through the curtained partition.

Who was she? What the hell had happened to her? She hadn't been seen by a doctor yet, but the nurse who had spoken briefly with Troy a few moments ago assured him that her injuries appeared to be minor, a few scrapes and bruises, nothing to warrant the amount of blood on her clothing. So whose blood was it? And how had it gotten on her?

As if reading his thoughts, Dermott said, "She's damn lucky that blood isn't hers. It's a wonder some drunk didn't splatter her all over the pavement."

Somehow *lucky* wasn't a word Troy would ascribe to the pale, frightened woman sitting on the very edge of the hospital bed, as if poised to flee the moment she sensed danger.

He wondered if she had any idea she was being watched. He and Dermott stood just outside the curtained partition, speaking loudly enough to be heard over the din of the ER and the storm that raged outside, but the woman gave no indication that she was aware of their presence. She sat stone still, staring at some distant point in space that only she seemed aware of.

He should have gone home, Troy decided wearily. His shift had ended hours ago, but he'd been delayed at the hospital with a prisoner who'd sustained serious injuries after a botched convenience-store holdup. Just as he was about to leave, hoping to beat the rain, his lieutenant had called him to tell him as long as he was still there he might as well stick around and talk to another suspect who was being brought in.

But the moment Troy had seen the blonde, he'd been experiencing a myriad of regrets. He didn't need this. Not tonight. He wished he'd told his lieutenant to go take a flying leap. Let somebody else handle this case. But it was too late now, and with another weary sigh, Troy pushed the curtain aside and stepped through.

He hardly made a sound, certainly nothing that could be heard over the groans in the next cubicle, but the woman's gaze shot up, panic flashing in her blue eyes before she glanced away, as if wanting to shield her emotions from him.

But in that moment when their eyes met, Troy felt an odd little tremor in the pit of his stomach, a sensation not unlike the ones he experienced in times of keen excitement or extreme danger.

Damn, he thought. He *really* didn't need this.

He walked toward her, but she didn't look at him again. Except for that brief moment of eye contact, she'd retreated into that distant place that made her appear so unreachable. So…fragile.

Troy guessed he ought to be relieved she wasn't his type. He didn't like fragile women. He wasn't like his brother, Ray, who needed to be in control, or his other brother, Mitch, who needed to be needed. Troy liked strong, secure, independent women. Women who knew the score as well as he did.

What he didn't like was a woman who brought out his protective instincts. He'd found out the hard way that a woman like that could be a dangerous thing for a man like him.

He cleared his throat, trying to draw her attention without causing her further alarm. "I'm Sergeant Stoner," he said gently. "I need to ask you a few questions."

When she didn't answer, he said, "Let's start with your name."

Still no response.

Taking out his notebook and pen, Troy tried not to let his eyes wander to the slender bare legs revealed by her short hemline. He concentrated instead on the bloodstains. "The nurse said you didn't appear to be seriously injured, but you have a lot of blood on your clothing. Can you tell me what happened?"

Silence.

Troy moved to the end of the bed, giving her a little more space. He studied her profile and wondered what she was thinking. He could almost feel her sinking deeper into that place where no one, least of all him, could reach her.

But he wanted to try anyway. He wanted to take her by those thin, tanned shoulders, gaze into those crystalline eyes and, by sheer force of will, bring her back to a place where he *could* reach her. Touch her...

He broke off his thoughts abruptly. "What were you doing out alone this time of night? Officer Dermott said he found you on Westheimer, walking down the middle of the street. What happened to you? Were you running away from someone? Were you assaulted?"

Her hands were clasped in her lap, and Troy saw they were trembling. He took that as a good sign. At least she wasn't completely unaffected by his questions.

A scream erupted down the hallway, and the woman flinched. She looked around, as if suddenly aware of her surroundings. The groans in the cubicle next to her grew louder, and her blue eyes widened in despair.

"Where am I?" she whispered.

"The emergency room at St. Mary's Hospital. Don't you remember?"

She looked around again, as if seeing the cubicle for the first time. Judging by the quality of her clothing and the heavy gold bracelet around her wrist, these stark surroundings were hardly the accommodations she was accustomed to. But she was damn lucky it was Sunday, Troy thought. On Friday and Saturday nights, beds were lined up in the hallway.

"What's your name?" he asked again.

She lapsed back into silence, her blue eyes again staring into space.

He walked toward her, recapping his pen and putting it away. "Look, I want to help you here. Your family must be worried sick about you—"

At the mention of the word *family,* her gaze darted up to his. Her eyes widened, giving her the appearance of an animal trapped in a headlight. Troy found himself leaning toward her, wanting to shield her from whatever terror had driven her out into the rainy darkness.

Her left hand fluttered to her neck, and for the first time, he saw the faint shadow of a bruise marring her forearm, as if someone had grabbed her roughly. He also saw the glitter of diamonds around the third finger of her left hand.

She was married, a suspect, completely off-limits. But before he could stop himself, Troy reached out to touch the bruise on her arm. She gasped and jerked away, wrapping her arms tightly around her middle as if she could somehow ward off whatever threat he might pose to her.

Troy let his hand drop to his side and said, "I won't hurt you. I only want to help you. Your husband...did he do that to you?"

The blue eyes flooded with tears, but she still said nothing.

Troy swore under his breath. He'd seen it before. A battered wife refusing to press charges against an abusive husband. Refusing to admit what had really happened until it was too late.

"Look," he said impatiently, running a hand through his damp hair, "I can't help you unless you level with me. Tell me what happened. What's your name? Where do you live?"

One tear spilled over and ran down her cheek. Troy had to forcibly restrain himself from reaching out to wipe it away. She looked so young, sitting there with a teardrop drying on her cheek and bloodstains drying on her dress.

Troy's temper surged at the thought of any man committing an act of violence against any woman, but especially one who was as defenseless as this one.

Or was she?

He let his gaze drift back to the bloodstains. "You don't have any identification on you. Did you lose your purse? Did someone steal it?" When she still didn't respond, he sighed. "This is getting us nowhere fast."

He started to turn away, but her blue gaze met his again, and in those crystal depths, he saw a plea for help that touched him all the way to his soul.

He took a step toward her in urgency. "Won't you at least tell me your name?"

"I...can't."

Her voice floated across the distance separating them and wrapped around him like a sweetly provocative perfume. Her blue eyes held him enthralled, mesmerizing him with the secrets hidden within. Troy had the sudden mental image of a gossamer spiderweb, so deceptively beautiful, so potentially deadly...

"What do you mean, you can't?" he asked. "Are you afraid to tell me your name?"

"I mean...I can't." Her voice quavered with emotion, and her eyes brimmed with tears. Troy thought he'd never seen a face so haunted. So terrified.

"I can't tell you my name," she whispered in anguish, "because I don't know it. I don't know who I am."

"HEY, DOC, WAIT UP!" Troy hurried to catch up with the man he'd been waiting to see.

Dr. Timothy Seavers, tall, lanky, with a plain face and a disarming smile, strode down the hospital corridor, his lab coat flapping behind him like the wings of some giant white bird. When he heard Troy's voice, he turned, the blue eyes behind the wire-rimmed glasses lighting up in recognition. "Troy! How's it going?" He pumped Troy's hand vigorously.

He hadn't seen him in years, but Troy had known Tim Seavers for a long time, ever since he'd attended medical school with Troy's younger sister, Madison.

"Not bad," Troy said. "How about you?"

"Busy. You know how it is." Tim ran a harried hand through his light brown hair. "So how's the family? Not a Sunday goes by I don't think about your mom's fried chicken."

"You should drop by sometime. She still cooks enough to feed a small army. She'd be thrilled to see you, and so would Dad. He's retired now, you know."

Tim's eyes widened in mock surprise. "You're kidding. I didn't think your old man would ever quit the force."

"Neither did I. Look, Tim, I need to talk to you about

the Jane Doe who was brought in earlier tonight. Blond hair, blue eyes, about so tall." Troy measured the air with his hand. "The one who says she doesn't remember her name."

Tim glanced at the chart in his hand. "What do you want to know?"

"I need for you to explain to me just exactly what her condition is. In layman's terms."

"She's only had a preliminary examination in the ER. None of the test results are back yet, including the blood work."

"I know all that," Troy said impatiently. "But you checked her out, right? What's your guess?"

Tim frowned. "I don't like to guess."

"Come on," Troy urged. "Just between you and me. Off the record. It would be a big help to me to know exactly what I'm dealing with here."

Tim sighed. "Okay. Like I said, I haven't seen all the test results yet, but my best guess, in layman's terms, is that she has hysterical amnesia."

"In other words, there's no physical reason for her memory loss? No bump on the head or anything like that?"

"Other than a few minor bruises, she appears to be perfectly healthy."

"She wasn't sexually assaulted, then?"

"No."

The woman's trauma, along with her almost palpable fear, had led Troy to the obvious conclusion. He felt a moment of intense relief before asking, "Is there any chance she could be faking the memory loss?"

Tim glanced at him curiously. "Anything's possible. It's also possible that by morning her memory may be restored, at least in part."

"Could the amnesia be drug related?"

"I can't say for sure until we get the blood work back, but I don't think so. I'm guessing she received a tremendous shock of some kind tonight, something so traumatic her mind couldn't cope, so she blocked out whatever it was she saw or heard."

"Or did," Troy added, almost to himself. "Her dress was covered in blood, and yet you say she only has minor injuries. The blood had to come from somewhere, Tim. From someone. I'll need that dress, by the way, along with the rest of her clothing."

Tim nodded. "I know the drill. We'll bag it up, along with all her other personal effects. That is, except for her wedding ring. She became quite agitated when the nurse tried to remove it. Under the circumstances, I felt it best not to upset her. Who knows? Her ring may be the one thing that can trigger her memory."

"Let's hope so." But Troy had a feeling it wasn't going to be that easy. "In the meantime, I'll get everything over to the lab. Hopefully, in a day or two we'll have some answers about Jane Doe one way or another."

"I feel sorry for her," Tim said suddenly. When Troy glanced at him in surprise, he shrugged. "I know. I'm a doctor. Like you cops, we aren't supposed to have feelings, but there's something…haunting about her. I can't explain it."

He didn't have to. Troy knew exactly what Tim meant, but he kept his opinion to himself. The last thing he needed was to be having feelings for a suspect, one who couldn't remember her own name, let alone how she'd come to be covered in blood. Troy had learned a long time ago that when it came to women, he was a lousy judge of character.

He said so long to Tim and then retraced his steps

down the hallway. After she'd been examined in the ER, the woman had been moved to a room on the seventh floor. Troy stood outside the door, wondering if he should go in and talk to her again. Demand some answers. Find out if she really was faking her amnesia.

But it was late, after one o'clock in the morning. The caffeine kick had long since worn off, and exhaustion was setting in. Troy couldn't remember how long it had been since he'd seen a bed. It seemed like a lifetime. He'd been working too damn hard, he thought. Seen too much going down lately. He didn't like closing his eyes anymore. Didn't like dreaming about the bullet that might have his name on it.

He wondered if his brother Gary, who had been killed in the line of duty five years ago, had had those same nightmares before he died. He wondered if Mitch and Ray, who were also cops, had them now, and knew he would be relieved to learn that they did.

But there was no way Troy would ever ask them. No way he would ever reveal to his brothers that being a cop sometimes scared him. He was the daredevil of the family. The thrill seeker. The Stoner who didn't give a damn about tomorrow. His brothers would be shocked and not a little disappointed to learn that Troy had nerves after all. And that he just might be losing them.

Maybe he wouldn't go home, he decided. Even on a Sunday night, there were still places where he could find plenty of warm bodies and lonely souls who would be willing to share a few drinks and whatever else he might crave. Maybe he'd just go drink himself into a stupor so that when he finally did fall asleep, the doubts would be held at bay. For a few hours of blessed oblivion, he wouldn't have to think about mortality and betrayal and the woman from his past who had almost killed him.

* * *

SHE WOKE UP, choking on a scream. Someone was leaning over her bed, whispering to her.

Her eyes flew open, straining to see in the darkness that surrounded her. A scent lingered. Something familiar.

Fear exploded inside her, and she bolted upright, sweat pouring down her back. Her heart pounded in terror as she peered into the darkness, afraid to call out, afraid to even breathe. Someone was in here. Someone who wanted to hurt her.

A flash of lightning revealed that she was alone. No one was lurking in the shadows, but her terror did not lessen. She had to get out of here. She had to run away. Find someplace to hide where they would never find her.

An image of a small, dark room appeared in her mind, and an overwhelming sense of panic engulfed her. She couldn't go back *there*. They would find her. They would lock that dark room and never let her out. They would say she'd done bad things. Terrible things.

But before she could get out of bed, light flooded her room, the door opened and a middle-aged nurse with a kindly face bustled into the room. "What's the matter, hon?"

She looked at the nurse blankly. "Wh-what?"

The nurse nodded toward the bed. "You pressed the call button several times. Do you need something? Are you in pain?"

She uncurled her fist and found the call button inside. She hadn't even been aware of holding it, much less pressing it to summon help. "I think someone was in here."

The nurse took her by the shoulders and pressed her gently back against the pillow. "You probably had a nightmare. God knows, this weather is enough to give anyone the heebie-jeebies."

It wasn't a nightmare. She was sure of it. Someone had been in here with her. Someone—or something—evil.

"Someone was here," she said again.

"No one was here," the nurse soothed. "I've been at the desk all night. I would have seen if anyone had come into your room."

What about the scent? she wanted to ask. But the fragrance, so tantalizingly familiar, had already faded away. She put her hands to her face. "What's wrong with me? Why can't I remember?" she whispered.

"You will," the nurse assured her. "The doctor said your tests so far all appear normal. More than likely, your memory loss is only temporary. In a few days, everything will start to come back to you."

No! She didn't want everything to come back to her. What if they took her away again? What if they locked her in that dark room again?

But even as those thoughts flitted through her mind, a flash of memory caught her by surprise. A man's voice screaming *Andrea!*

Her heart started to pound again. "Andrea," she murmured. "My name is Andrea."

The nurse brightened. "There, you see? You're starting to remember already. What you need now is rest." She straightened the covers with an economy of motion. "Do you want me to bring you something to help you sleep?"

No drugs! The idea filled her with terror.

The nurse patted her arm. "Very well, then. Do you need anything else before I go?"

I need to know why I'm so afraid! I need to know who wants me dead!

She needed to know about the dark room.

But she said nothing.

"Get some sleep now," the nurse said, turning toward the door. "Everything will seem better in the morning."

But Andrea didn't think so. She didn't think daylight would bring an end to her terror.

Chapter Two

When she awakened again, sunlight streamed in through the hospital window. She closed her eyes and lay there, hovering pleasantly between sleep and wakefulness. She'd been dreaming about Mayela. The two of them were walking in the park, laughing and talking and having a wonderful time. She always had a wonderful time with Mayela—

Who is Mayela? a voice in the back of her mind asked.

And with that question, the terror of last night returned. She sat up in bed and gazed around frantically. Where was she?

The hospital. She dimly remembered being brought to the emergency room. She'd talked to a police officer, hadn't she?

Her hand flew to her mouth. Oh, God, what had she told him? What if he found out about the dark room? About all the blood? What if he sent her back? What if—?

You didn't tell him anything, the little voice assured her. *Because you don't remember anything.*

There was safety in not remembering.

She did a quick survey of the room. A window, one

door that led to the hallway, another door that led to the bathroom and a sink with a mirror.

Andrea got up and padded over to the window. The parking lot was far below. No one could have gotten into her room through the window. She crossed to the door and peeked out. The elevators were at the end of the hallway, near the nurses' station. No one could have come that way without being seen. The nurse had been right. The intruder last night had been nothing more than a product of Andrea's imagination. But somehow that thought did not make her feel any better. Far from it.

She let the door close and moved to the sink to examine her reflection in the mirror. Blond hair, blue eyes, oval face, full lips, high cheekbones. A model's face, she thought without pride, for the face in the mirror belonged to a stranger. *Was* she a model? A wife? A mother? Was that who Mayela was? Her child?

But surely she would be able to remember her own child. What kind of mother would forget her child?

And her husband? She searched her mind frantically for an image, then lifted her left hand to stare dispassionately at the impressive glitter of diamonds in the mirror. If she had a husband and a child out there somewhere, why did she feel so lost? So lonely? Why did she feel as if she didn't belong anywhere?

Why wasn't her husband looking for her? Why hadn't he come forward to claim her?

A sudden explosion of memory caught her by surprise. A voice deep inside her mind screamed, *I hate you. I want you dead.*

A red mist covered her vision.

Andrea's right hand curled at her side, as if gripping a knife. She lifted the imaginary blade to the mirror and struck at her reflection.

I hate you. I want you dead. Dead! Dead! Dead!

Gasping in horror, Andrea grabbed her right wrist with her left hand as if to physically restrain the slashing motion. What had happened to her?

What had she done?

BY MIDMORNING, she had been poked, prodded, X-rayed, stuck with needles, her blood drawn, her head examined, her vital signs checked and rechecked, and all because she couldn't seem to remember who she was.

"Well, Andrea, I have good news and I have bad news," Dr. Seavers announced as he strode into her hospital room later that day. "The good news is, I can't find anything wrong with you."

"And the bad news?"

"I can't find anything wrong with you." He pulled up a chair beside her bed and sat down. "The MRI and the CAT scan have turned up nil, and the blood work so far is clean, which is pretty much what I expected. Your memory loss appears to be psychosomatic."

"Meaning I can't remember because I don't want to." She studied the doctor carefully.

He took off his glasses and rubbed the bridge of his nose with his thumb and forefinger. "It's usually not quite that simple."

Wasn't it? "Will I ever remember?"

He slipped back on his glasses, gazing at her with earnest blue eyes. "There are no guarantees, of course, but I'd say the chances are excellent your memory will return."

"All of it?"

"Probably not all at once. Bits and pieces will come back to you, sudden flashes maybe. Eventually you may remember everything."

"When?"

"That's what I'd like to know," said another voice from the doorway. Andrea's eyes darted to the figure standing just inside her room. He looked vaguely familiar, but she couldn't place him. There was something disturbing about the way his dark eyes studied her so intently. Something frightening about the way she seemed to respond to him.

For a moment, she wondered if he might be her husband. Was that why he seemed so familiar to her? A thrill of excitement raced up her back. A memory darted through her mind.

A man was kissing her. A man just as tall and dark and handsome as this man.

But he wasn't this man.

Disappointment shot through her as she quickly tore her gaze from his.

Dr. Seavers said, "You remember Sergeant Stoner?"

The policeman who'd questioned her last night. *I don't like cops,* she thought suddenly, though she had no idea why.

She flashed him another glance, and he smiled at her. Andrea's pulse fluttered in her throat. He really was quite attractive, she thought, and wondered why she hadn't noticed last night.

Maybe she had noticed. Maybe she'd forgotten.

She didn't see how she could forget this man, though.

But she'd forgotten her husband.

I want you dead!

She looked away, unable to hold Sergeant Stoner's probing gaze.

"I'm glad to see you're looking so much better this morning." He crossed the room to her bed.

Dr. Seavers stood up. "I'll stop by later, and we can talk more. I'm sure you still have a lot of questions."

"As do I." Something in Sergeant Stoner's voice made Andrea tense, and she realized that his smile had only been a ruse. He wasn't to be trusted after all.

"Have you remembered anything?" he asked when Dr. Seavers had left the room.

"My name." She was still unable to meet his gaze. "It's Andrea."

"So I heard. That's a very pretty name." He paused, then said, "And your last name?"

"I don't know." Andrea didn't know why she felt so afraid to look at him. Guilt, maybe? Was she afraid he would see something in her eyes that even she didn't know about?

She wondered if she should tell him about the intruder in her room last night. But why should he believe her when Andrea wasn't even sure herself? He might think her crazy. He might want to send her to the dark room.

"What's wrong? Have you remembered something else?"

"No, nothing." With an effort, Andrea willed herself to relax, forced her gaze to meet Sergeant Stoner's. His eyes were a dark, impenetrable brown and fringed with long, curly lashes. He was tall and lean, but Andrea knew that beneath his suit coat, the muscles in his arms and chest would be powerful. She could almost feel them flex and bunch beneath her hands—

She stopped her thoughts cold. Was she remembering how it felt to be in a man's arms? Or was she experiencing wishful thinking, because of this particular man?

Just what kind of woman are *you?*

Obviously one who wasn't to be believed, she thought,

if the shadow of doubt in Sergeant Stoner's eyes was any indication.

"Let's go back to last night," he said. "What's the first thing you remember?"

Andrea closed her eyes, straining for recall. "The emergency room. There was so much noise. Someone screamed."

"Do you remember talking to me?"

She flicked him a sidelong glance. "Vaguely."

"Do you remember being examined?"

A blush of humiliation touched her cheeks. The examination had been thorough. "Yes."

"Dr. Seavers said he could find nothing physically wrong with you."

"So he told me."

"Your amnesia appears to be—"

"Fake?"

Something flashed in those brown eyes. "I didn't say that."

"But you have your doubts about me, don't you? I can tell."

"I'm not a doctor, I'm a cop. We tend to see things in black-and-white. We're naturally wary of terms like 'hysterical amnesia' and 'psychosomatic.'"

Hysterical amnesia? *Was* she hysterical? Andrea didn't think so. Right now, she felt amazingly calm. Completely in control. She began to relax because she knew as good a detective as Sergeant Stoner might be, he wouldn't find out anything she didn't want him to.

"Do you have any idea why you might have been walking down the middle of a busy street at ten o'clock at night in a thunderstorm?" he asked suddenly.

Andrea's poise slipped a little. She shook her head.

"Were you trying to get away from someone?"

That struck a note of truth, but Andrea forced her expression to remain placid. Safety lay in keeping her mind a blank. She shook her head again.

Sergeant Stoner took a deliberate step toward her. He towered over the side of her bed, and his dark eyes probed her face, searching for the truth. "Where did all that blood come from, Andrea?"

"Wh-what?"

He bent toward her, his eyes intense. Andrea found she wasn't quite as calm as she'd thought. "You had blood all over your clothing, but it wasn't yours. Whose blood was it?"

"I—I don't know."

Sergeant Stoner stared down at her. "You have to admit, your memory loss seems just a little too convenient. You're found wandering down a busy street in the middle of the night, covered in blood. Yet you can't remember why you were on that street or how that blood got on your clothing. You can't even remember your last name. Our hands are tied, Andrea. We don't know if a crime has been committed or not. We don't even know where to start looking. And if a crime was committed, by the time your memory returns, the trail will have undoubtedly grown cold. Do you see what I mean?"

She saw, all right. She knew exactly what he was driving at. "Just what is it you think I've done?"

"I don't know." He sat down in the chair next to her bed and took out a black fountain pen, twirling it between his fingers. "All I know is that you had a great deal of blood on your clothing when you were brought to this hospital. Type O-positive, the lab tells me. Does that mean anything to you?"

"No. I don't even know what type my own blood is."

"It's A-negative, as a matter of fact."

"It seems you know more about me than I know about myself." She didn't think she was usually so flip, but Sergeant Stoner frightened her, and she had to hide behind something.

"I doubt that," he replied. "I doubt that very much."

When she didn't answer, he tried another tack. "Would you be willing to talk to a psychiatrist?"

An image of the dark room rose in her mind, and Andrea's heart pounded in terror. *No!*

She didn't want to talk to a psychiatrist. That was the last thing in the world she wanted.

She forced herself to stare at him coolly. "Will my talking to a psychiatrist alleviate your doubts about my amnesia?"

He shrugged noncommittally. "Will you talk to her?"

"Her?"

"Someone I know. She's very good. You'll like her."

"I suppose I'll have to take your word for that, won't I?" Andrea said, wondering just who the woman was and what she meant to Sergeant Stoner.

Those dark eyes studied her carefully. "You do want to remember, don't you?"

"Of course I do. Why wouldn't I?"

"That's a good question, Andrea. A very good question."

TROY FROWNED as he stood in the hallway outside her hospital room. The interview hadn't gone quite as he'd expected. She was too damn cool, for one thing. What had happened to the poor, helpless girl he'd seen in the ER last night? The woman he'd just spoken with seemed completely in control of her faculties, and not nearly frightened or confused enough for someone who couldn't remember her own name.

A chill of foreboding crept up Troy's spine. What kind of game was she playing? And what the hell did it have to do with him?

WHAT DO YOU THINK you're doing, Andrea? The woman with the haunted blue eyes stared back at her in the mirror.

I couldn't let him see how much he frightened me. Then he would know something was wrong.

He already knows something is wrong, her reflection scolded. *You were found wandering down a busy street with blood all over your clothing, and you don't remember who you are or what happened to you. What is he supposed to think?*

That I'm guilty.

Of what?

I don't know.

Yes, you do. You know. You know.

She raised her left hand and stared at the diamonds twinkling on her finger.

I want you dead! Dead! Dead! Dead!

"THE LAB FOUND TRACES of a mild sedative in her bloodstream," Tim said.

"A sedative?" Troy frowned. "What do you make of that?"

"Parvonal C is sometimes used in sleeping medications, completely harmless in the amount we found in Andrea's blood. It might have contributed to her disorientation, but it wouldn't have caused her memory loss. Everything else appears normal. Under the circumstances, I won't be able to keep her here much longer. We're just too understaffed and too short on beds."

''Where will she go?'' Troy asked, but he knew the answer as well as Tim did.

Tim shrugged, not in indifference, but in resignation. ''Judging by her clothing and jewelry, she doesn't appear to be destitute. Maybe someone in her family will turn up to claim her. If not, there's always the shelters.''

Troy tried to picture Andrea in one of the homeless shelters downtown, but the image was too incongruous. She obviously didn't belong in a shelter, but just where did she belong? So far no one had filed a missing-persons report fitting her description, and Troy was having a hard time believing that no one in her family had missed her yet. But it hadn't even been twenty-four hours. Andrea's husband might yet turn up to claim her.

And what if he did claim her? What if he was the reason Andrea had been found wandering alone at night, bruised, disoriented and frightened? What then? Troy would have no recourse but to turn her over to him. If Andrea couldn't remember what had happened, if she couldn't file a complaint against him, there would be nothing Troy could do to help her.

What makes you think she wants your help? Or needs it, for that matter? he asked himself as he thought about the cool, collected woman he'd spoken with earlier. It was almost as if he'd interviewed two very different people. One vulnerable and frightened, one calm and controlled.

He wasn't sure which one of them was the true Andrea. Or which one of them was the most dangerous.

''I'd like Madison to talk with her,'' he said. ''Do you have any objections?''

Surprise flashed in Tim's red-rimmed eyes. ''I have no objections. In fact, it'll be nice to see your sister again.''

* * *

IT WAS LATE AFTERNOON and Andrea had just awakened from a troubled sleep. She'd dreamed about Mayela again. The name had been fresh on her mind when she'd opened her eyes, but when she'd tried to put a face with the name, the tenuous image vanished.

Was Mayela even a real person or another figment of her imagination?

A knock sounded on her door, and she called out, "Come in," expecting to see either Dr. Seavers or one of the nurses. But the dark-haired young woman who stuck her head around the door was someone Andrea was sure she'd never seen before.

"Hello," the woman said pleasantly. "Up for a little visit?"

Andrea shrugged, immediately on guard. But the woman's smile was infectious, and Andrea soon found her uneasiness fading. The woman was tall, at least five-eight or five-nine, and very slender, with short, glossy black hair and dark brown eyes that tipped slightly at the corners. She wore faded jeans, a yellow T-shirt and a pair of running shoes that had definitely seen better days.

"I'm Madison Stoner," she said. "It seems we have a mutual acquaintance."

Andrea looked at her in surprise. "You mean Sergeant Stoner? Are you his wife?"

The brown eyes twinkled. "No, thank God. I'm his sister, which might have just as many disadvantages, come to think of it." She set her macramé bag in the chair and came to stand beside Andrea's bed. Not too close, though. She was careful to keep an unthreatening distance, Andrea noted.

"You're the psychiatrist he told me about," she said with sudden insight.

Dr. Stoner gave her a mock frown. "Am I that transparent?"

Was she? Andrea wasn't sure how she'd identified the woman so quickly. How she had associated that calm voice and nonjudgmental expression with those of a psychiatrist.

She'll lock you in the dark room if you're not careful. "I don't know what your brother told you, but I'm not crazy," Andrea said, moistening her dry lips. "I just can't remember."

Dr. Stoner smiled sympathetically. "Yes, I know. That must be pretty scary."

Scary? Her amnesia was terrifying, but Andrea knew remembering would be worse. Remembering would be the death of her.

She couldn't afford to let Dr. Stoner help her regain her memory, and she couldn't let Sergeant Stoner suspect her resistance. It was all so tricky, this deception. So nerve-racking. Andrea felt the onslaught of a terrific headache. She massaged her temples with her fingertips.

"Are you in pain, Andrea?"

"No, I'm okay."

"You sure? I could ring for the nurse."

"No, I'm fine. Just tired."

"I won't stay long," Dr. Stoner assured her with another warm smile. "But as long as I'm here, we might as well get acquainted. Do you mind if I sit?"

"Of course not."

Dr. Stoner tossed her purse onto the floor and sat. "So." She crossed her long legs and smiled at Andrea. "What do you think of my brother?"

The question was so unexpected that Andrea found herself blurting out the truth. "He's very good-looking."

Madison laughed. "You aren't the first woman to have noticed that. He's quite the lady-killer, my brother."

Andrea wondered what Sergeant Stoner would say if he could hear the way his sister talked about him to a complete stranger. Dr. Stoner wasn't like any psychiatrist Andrea had ever known, but then, she had no idea how many she had known.

She fingered her wedding band. "Is...he married?"

"Troy? Please. He has an aversion to commitment. But then, all the Stoners seem to suffer from that affliction. None of my other brothers are married, either."

"How many brothers do you have?"

"Three. Ray's the oldest, then Mitch, and then Troy. They're all cops, and so is my dad. Or he was, until he retired last month. Can you imagine what my social life has been like?" She laughed without rancor, and her brown eyes tilted even more.

"An entire family of cops," Andrea murmured. The notion intrigued her for some reason.

"Oh, you have no idea. My family's fascination with law enforcement goes back a long way. Both of my grandfathers were police officers, and one of my great-grandmothers was a county sheriff," she said with obvious pride.

"Why didn't you go into law enforcement?" Andrea asked.

A wistful smile touched Dr. Stoner's lips. "I almost did. Up until I went to college, I had every intention of following in the Stoner tradition."

"What happened?"

The smile disappeared. "Oh...that's a long story. Anyway, I've found being a psychiatrist has its distinct advantages in my family. My brothers usually steer clear of me because they're afraid I'll try to psychoanalyze them. No cop can stand that.''

Andrea glanced at Dr. Stoner's hands folded in her lap. Her fingers were long and graceful, like those of a pianist, and unadorned with rings. ''You aren't married, either, then?''

''No. But I see that you wear a wedding band. It's very beautiful,'' Dr. Stoner said.

The transition was made so skillfully, Andrea was hardly aware of it. She lifted her hand and studied the diamonds.

''You don't remember your husband, do you?'' Dr. Stoner asked softly. ''That must be very troubling.''

If you only knew.

''Have you had any flashes of memory at all?''

A dark room. A knife. Someone named Mayela. What did it all mean? ''I don't think so,'' Andrea said. ''At least nothing that makes any sense.''

''It probably won't for a while. Everything will seem hazy at first, but then your memories will become clearer and clearer until eventually, everything will click back into place.''

''You make it sound like a puzzle.''

''It is, in a way. Almost all of the pieces are missing right now, but as you find each piece, the bigger picture will start to take shape.''

''How do I find the missing pieces?'' Andrea asked fearfully.

''You may not have to. They may find you. But if they don't, there are certain procedures that might help you.''

''Such as?''

''Regressive hypnosis, for one thing.''

''*Hypnosis?*'' Why was that idea so terrifying? Because she was afraid to remember what had happened? What she might have done? Andrea shivered.

"Does the idea of hypnosis disturb you, Andrea?"

"No, it's just…"

Dr. Stoner smiled. "I understand. Everything is very confusing for you right now. But try not to worry. I'm willing to bet your memory will return on its own in a few days. All you need is a little time."

But how much time did she have? Andrea wondered. How much time before they found her?

Who's they? her mind screamed in frustration.

Dr. Stoner picked up her purse and stood. "I can see you're getting tired. Why don't I let you get some rest and we'll talk again later. That is, if you want me to come back." When Andrea hesitated, she said, "It wouldn't have to be as a psychiatrist, you know. I could come back as a friend."

Sudden tears filled Andrea's eyes. The loneliness and fear were suddenly overwhelming. A deep despair settled over her. "I'd like that," she said, almost in a whisper. "I think I could use a friend right now."

Chapter Three

Forty-eight hours had passed, and still no missing-persons report had come in on anyone fitting Andrea's description. Lieutenant Lucas seemed particularly put out by this turn of events.

"We need to get this thing cleared up, Stoner. I don't like loose ends."

"I'm all over it, sir," Troy assured his superior on Wednesday morning. "I've got the lab reports right here, but unfortunately they're not all that useful at the moment. We don't have any unsolved homicides in the last two days with type O-positive blood, so for the moment, that's a dead end. Her dress, however, is by a fairly unknown but pricey designer whose label is only carried in two stores here in Houston. I'm going in to talk with the managers this afternoon."

"What about her jewelry?"

"I've taken the bracelet around to a few upscale jewelry stores that specialize in custom pieces, but no luck so far."

"She was also wearing a wedding band, right? Any leads on that?"

Troy looked away. "Uh, no. Actually she's still wearing the ring. She got pretty upset when the nurse tried to remove it, so under the circumstances, her doctor felt it best to let her wear it. He thinks her ring may be the one thing that can trigger her memory.''

Lucas scowled. ''Might be an inscription inside, though. Have you thought about that?''

Of course Troy had thought about that. *To My Beloved Wife...*

He shrugged. ''When her doctor says the time is right, I'll ask her to take off the ring.''

Lucas nodded. ''Well, stay on it. I want this thing cleaned up.'' He dropped a stack of folders on Troy's desk. ''We've got bigger problems than some chick who can't remember her own address.''

Troy didn't figure it necessary to point out the fact that that same ''chick'' might have been involved in a crime. That there might be a little more going on with Andrea whatever-her-name-turned-out-to-be than just memory loss.

But he didn't say anything. He didn't want Lieutenant Lucas thinking he might have a little more interest in this case than was warranted. He didn't want Lucas remembering the rumors about Troy's involvement with a certain murder suspect named Cassandra Markham, and he sure as hell didn't want Lucas remembering how that involvement had almost cost Troy his badge. Not to mention his life.

Five years ago, right after Troy had first made detective, the Markham case had been his first major homicide investigation. Cassandra Markham had been the chief suspect in her husband's murder, but her sweet smile, her youth and naiveté had convinced Troy she was innocent.

His brother Gary had just been killed a month earlier, and looking back, Troy guessed he'd been vulnerable. And gullible. He'd fallen in love with Cassandra Markham, and she'd played him for the fool he was. He'd learned the hard way that looks, more often than not, were deceiving, and he'd vowed he would never make that same mistake again.

And yet here he was, attracted to another suspect.

But he was older now and wiser, and a hell of a lot more cynical. It would take more than killer blue eyes and soft blond hair to turn his head this time.

BY THE END of the third day, Andrea was becoming accustomed to her memory loss. She no longer awakened frightened and disoriented, and she found herself looking forward to Sergeant Stoner's visits in a way she didn't understand. She instinctively knew he could be dangerous to her, and yet the effect he had on her was undeniable.

Of course, there was no way she could ever let Sergeant Stoner—Troy, as she had begun to think of him— know of her feelings. He'd remained so aloof, so impersonal with her that she knew he only thought of her as a suspect.

And therein lay the danger. He thought of her as a *suspect*. Someone who may have committed a terrible crime. If he had even an inkling of her feelings for him, he would question her motives even more. He would begin to wonder what kind of woman would be married to one man and attracted to another.

A woman who couldn't be trusted, that's who.

And she needed him to trust her. If she were to have any chance at all, she had to somehow make him believe in her.

She got up and padded to the mirror, gazing critically at her reflection. She looked much better today, with her hair clean and combed, and a touch of makeup complementing her features. Madison—as Dr. Stoner had insisted she call her—had dropped by earlier this morning and brought Andrea a pale blue silk nightgown along with an assortment of toiletries and cosmetics. Andrea had been overwhelmed by the generosity and thoughtfulness of the gift. It was amazing what getting out of a hospital gown could do for one's spirits.

But as she walked to the window and stared out at the early-afternoon rain, her spirits once again sagged. Did she have a family out there somewhere, loved ones who were waiting anxiously for some word of her whereabouts? Why hadn't they come forward, then? Why hadn't they been looking for her? Was there no one out there who missed her? Who cared about her?

Loneliness tugged at her heart, the emotion all too familiar. Instinctively she knew she'd experienced this feeling before. The sensation settled around her like an old, comfortable shawl. She'd learned to deal with her loneliness years ago, hadn't she? When she'd lost her mother and father. When she'd been sent to that dark room—

The door of her hospital room opened, and Andrea swung around. It was the first time she'd faced Troy, standing up, and she wished that it made her feel less vulnerable to him, but the impact was the same. Her heart beat an excited staccato inside her.

"I'm sorry," he said. "I knocked, but I guess you didn't hear me."

She lifted her chin, swinging her long hair over one shoulder in a move she hoped appeared casual. "It's okay. Come in."

He let the door close behind him, but his eyes never left her. Suddenly she realized he was seeing the differences in her, too. The blue silk nightgown, the combed hair, the makeup. His gaze was oddly intense.

She picked up a fold of the nightgown. "Your sister came by this morning and brought me a CARE package. I feel like a new woman."

"Madison's thoughtful that way." His gaze lingered just a fraction too long on the delicate lace neckline of her gown.

"She's very nice," Andrea agreed, wondering if her voice sounded as breathless to him as it did to her. "You were right. I like her a lot."

"Good. I'm hoping she'll be able to help you. In the meantime, I may have a lead."

A fist of panic closed over Andrea's throat. Her hand crept to the tender skin on her arm, where the bruise was now almost invisible. "What kind of lead?"

"Your dress." His gaze dropped for a fraction of a second to the nightgown she wore. "The label is from a designer whose line is carried in only two stores in Houston. Alaina's in the Village and Zoë's on Post Oak near the Pavilion. Both shops are fairly small but very exclusive. Do either of those names ring a bell for you?"

Andrea closed her eyes, searching her mind. Her dress was a designer original from an expensive shop, and she knew that the heavy, ornate bracelet the police had taken from her the first night in the hospital was solid gold, worth a small fortune, as was the diamond wedding band that sparkled on her finger. Her nails bore the evidence of a professional manicure, and her long hair was so precisely cut that every strand fell into place by a simple shake of her head.

And yet...she didn't feel rich. She didn't feel pampered. Far from it. Andrea had the distinct impression that she had worked very hard all of her life. That at times mere survival had been an extraordinary struggle.

So where did her expensive jewelry and clothing come from? A wealthy husband?

The memory came so blindingly fast that Andrea had no time to prepare herself. She saw him so clearly, an older man with gray hair and a careworn face. *I'm a rich man, Andrea. As my wife, you will be entitled to certain privileges, anything your heart desires....*

You little gold digger! Who do you think you're fooling? I'll see you in hell before you get a penny of his money!

I want you to know that I've changed my will, Andrea. When my time comes, you will be well taken care of.

I hate you. I want you dead!

In her mind's eye, Andrea saw the gray-haired man fall to the floor, blood gushing from the stab wounds in his chest.

Andrea's knees buckled as she followed her vision to the floor.

SHE WEIGHED no more than a dream. Troy lifted her easily and carried her to the bed. As he bent over to lay her on top of the sheets, a strand of her hair curled around his arm, and once again the image of a spiderweb formed in his mind. But he shook it off and reached for the call button.

The nurse, an enormous Hispanic woman with hips the size of a battleship, stormed in and hustled Troy out of the way. She quickly felt Andrea's pulse and took her vital signs, all the while muttering in Spanish under her breath, something that Troy thought translated roughly to, "Stupid cops. Stupid men. God give me strength."

She removed the stethoscope from her ears and glanced at Troy. "She fainted." Her voice was distinctly accusing. "What did you do to her?"

"Nothing."

"She faint for no reason? I don't think so. Women don't faint for no reason. Men maybe, not women."

"I didn't do anything to her," Troy said. "We were just talking."

The nurse's dark eyes narrowed on him. "Cops like to talk too damn much, I think. Now, get out of my way," she said as Troy started toward the bed. She lifted both hands as if to shove him back, and Troy retreated a safe distance away.

"Is she going to be all right?"

"Maybe, if you let her rest." She pulled the sheet over Andrea and tucked it about her shoulders.

"I'm just trying to do my job," he said defensively.

She gave him a "Humph" that told him exactly what she thought of his job.

Andrea moaned and her eyes fluttered open. The nurse's expression immediately softened. It was amazing how quickly Andrea had managed to assemble her troops. *She'd* come into the hospital covered in someone else's blood, and Troy was suddenly the villain of the piece.

"What happened?" she murmured.

"You fainted," the nurse said gently as she lifted Andrea's wrist and felt her pulse again. "Almost back to normal."

Andrea's brows drew together. "I...fainted?"

"Yeah," Troy said, coming to stand by her bedside. "You gave me quite a scare."

Andrea's gaze flew to his, as if she'd forgotten his presence. He said quickly, "You seemed to have remembered something that upset you."

She lifted a hand to her forehead. "I just felt so weak suddenly. So dizzy..."

"I think it was more than that," Troy insisted.

The nurse shot him a warning glance. "She needs her rest."

"If I go now, I'll just have to come back later. Wouldn't you rather get our talk over with?" he asked Andrea.

"I don't remember anything. What more is there to say?" She turned her head toward the window.

"Oh, I think we'll find something to talk about."

The nurse shook her finger at him. "Ten minutes, no more. You understand me?" She marched across the room and opened the door. "I'll be back," she said in a voice that sounded alarmingly like Arnold Schwarzenegger with a Spanish accent.

When the door closed behind her, Troy turned back to Andrea. "You've got yourself quite a champion there. Do you always make friends this quickly?"

Andrea frowned at his tone. "I don't know what you mean."

Troy shrugged. "You seem to have a knack for making people want to go out of their way to help you. My sister, Dr. Seavers, the nurses." Who else had she put under her spell?

"Is that a crime, Sergeant Stoner?" Her beguiling blue eyes, even more startling against her now pale face, trapped him with her stare. He couldn't look away and Troy found himself wondering if he was becoming her next victim.

In a bloodstained dress with wet, matted hair, she'd been dangerous enough, but in a blue silk nightgown that was hardly more than imagination, and her hair—an intriguing shade of silvery gold—curling down her back, Troy thought her positively lethal. She was a knockout, a woman that would be noticed in a crowd of beautiful women, and yet no one had come forward to identify her. No one had reported her missing. Why?

It didn't make sense. Nothing about this woman made sense, least of all the way his body was responding to her in that blue silk nightgown.

"What did you want to talk to me about, Sergeant?" Andrea asked softly.

Her voice sent a shiver of unease up Troy's spine. He deliberately turned away from her and walked over to the window. The drizzle of early afternoon had turned into a full-fledged downpour. He could hardly see beyond the parking lot.

"Are you in the habit of taking sleeping pills?"

"What?"

He turned back to her. Her eyes were wide with shock. "Dr. Seavers said the lab found trace amounts of a mild sedative in your blood, a drug called Parvonal C. It's usually found in over-the-counter sleeping medications."

Andrea frowned. "I don't think I would take sleeping pills."

"But you can't know that for sure, can you? Since you can't remember?"

Their gazes met and held almost in challenge, and then Andrea glanced away. "No." She took a deep breath and released it. "Is that what you wanted to talk to me about?"

"There's something else," Troy said. "I'd like to run a picture of you in the newspapers and on television. There must be a reason why your family hasn't come forward. Maybe they don't realize you're missing."

"How could they not know?" Her blue gaze tracked him as he turned away from the window. "It's been days. If there was someone out there who cared about me—"

she fingered her wedding ring "—he would have already come forward, wouldn't he?"

Although it was hard to argue with her logic, Troy found it even more difficult to believe a woman like her would have no one. "Not necessarily. There are any number of reasons why you might not have been missed. Your husband may be away. Or he may think *you're* away. The best way to get the answers we need is to run the picture."

"Dr. Seavers and Madison both agree that my memory will probably return on its own in time."

"But how much time?"

Her gaze dropped.

Troy stepped close to her bed, staring down at her. "I don't think we *have* that kind of time, Andrea. I don't know how to explain it, but I feel some urgency in this matter. I think we need to find out who you are and what happened to you as soon as possible." It was imperative, in fact, that he return her to her real life, to her husband, before it was too late.

Before he, too, got caught in her web.

"I'M SERGEANT STONER," he said, showing his ID and badge to a clerk who appeared to be no more than seventeen or eighteen. "I'd like to talk to the owner."

The girl look unimpressed by the badge. "Zoë's my aunt."

Which probably explained how a girl who wore black lipstick and nail polish, not to mention hot pants and white retro boots, managed to snare a job in a swanky joint like this. She looked like an escapee from the seventies, and Troy wondered what kind of familial persuasion had been brought to bear on poor Zoë to give the girl a job. "Is your aunt here?"

The girl examined the black nails, which were so long they'd begun to curl under, giving her hands the appearance of claws. "She's out of town and won't be back until the end of the week."

"What about the manager?"

"Called away on a family emergency. No one's here but me."

"Are you in charge, then?" Troy asked carefully.

She shrugged. "Yeah, I guess so."

"I called yesterday about a particular dress you carry here. I talked to someone named Carol."

"She's the manager, but she's not here."

"So you said. Look, I'm going to need your help…"

"Star," she supplied, flipping back her straight, white blond hair. "My name's Star."

"Star, the dress I'm looking for is by a designer named Tamara Casey, and I'm told Zoë's is one of two shops here in Houston that carry her line." He'd already bombed out at Alaina's, the shop in the Village, and was hoping for better luck here. "Are you familiar with that designer?"

Star shuddered. "We carry Tamara Casey, all right, but I wouldn't be caught dead in any of her clothes."

Troy fervently hoped Star wasn't planning on making sales her lifelong career. "The dress I'm looking for is short, white, sleeveless. Real nice. Do you know the one I mean?"

"Maybe." The girl tucked a strand of hair behind an ear that was pierced no less than five times. She led him to the front of the store and pulled a dress from the rack. "Is this it?"

Troy fingered the fine fabric, remembering the way that dress had looked on Andrea. Remembering the bloodstains. "That's the one."

"We've only had this style a few days," the girl told him. "If it was purchased in here, it had to have been since last week."

"That should make tracing the purchaser a little easier," Troy said.

Star shrugged. "Yes and no. If the dress was charged to an account, Carol could probably use the computer when she comes back to find out who bought it, but if someone paid cash for it…" She shrugged again in dismissal.

"Does that happen often?" Troy asked. "Someone paying cash? I didn't think that was done much anymore."

"It is if some rich old geezer doesn't want his wife snooping in his business."

In other words, men buying presents for their mistresses wouldn't want a record of the transaction that their wives might run across.

"I see what you mean." Troy fished in his coat pocket for a card. He handed it to Star. "Why don't you give me a call when your aunt gets back from her trip or Carol gets back from her emergency?"

"Sure." The girl glanced at his card. "There's not like a, you know, a reward or anything involved, is there?"

FOUR DAYS AFTER she'd been found and brought to the hospital, Andrea's picture was shown on TV. She was watching the news when she first saw it. One moment they were talking about a tropical storm in the gulf that had just been upgraded to a hurricane, and then in the next instant, the radar map gave way to her picture with the lead-in, "The police are searching for the identity of this woman…."

Andrea stared at her picture, trembling uncontrollably.

The fear that had been kept under control came storming back, stunning her with its intensity.

She should never have let her picture be shown on TV. But how could she have stopped it without arousing Troy's suspicions? She knew he already doubted her. She couldn't afford to make him even more suspicious. She needed him on her side. When everything came out—

It won't. As long as your memory is lost, no one will find out anything.

But how long could she keep the memories at bay?

How long could she keep pretending she was an innocent victim?

Chapter Four

It was dark by the time Troy got back to the hospital to see Andrea. She was sleeping with the light on, and Troy flipped off the switch, letting the soft illumination from the corridor filter in. He started to turn away, but something about the way she stirred in her sleep drew him to her bed. He stood in the dark, staring down at her, wondering what secrets her dreams would reveal if he could see them. Wondering if he would ever find out the truth about her.

She muttered something in her sleep, a name, and Troy stepped closer. Her head thrashed from side to side. She was obviously in the throes of a powerful nightmare. Troy took her hand and shook it lightly.

Her eyes opened wide and she screamed, bolting upright in bed. She slashed out with one hand. "No! Please don't lock the door! It's so dark in here—"

Troy caught her thrashing arm in his hand. He tried to calm her. "Andrea, it's me, Troy. It's okay."

Her frantic movements ceased. "Troy?"

"Sergeant Stoner."

She clung to his hand. "I'm so glad to see you. I thought—" Her grip tightened. "Why is it so dark in here?"

"I turned off the light. I thought you might sleep better in the dark."

"I hate the dark!"

"Yeah, I got that. I'm sorry."

He was about to ask her why she was so afraid of the dark when the door to her room burst open, and a deep, masculine voice demanded, "What's goin' on in here?"

The light came on, and Troy found himself staring into the angry face of a burly male orderly. The man's eyes narrowed. "Who the hell are you?"

"Sergeant Stoner, HPD. Who the hell are you?"

He ignored Troy's question. "Is this man botherin' you, Miss Andrea?"

"No, it's okay, Calvin. He's a policeman. He's here to help me. Aren't you, Sergeant Stoner?"

Her gaze was a bit too challenging. Troy frowned. "I'm doing my damnedest."

"Well, you sure do have a funny way of helpin', that's all I know. Comin' in here, gettin' Miss Andrea all upset." Calvin's gaze went past Troy to fix on Andrea. "You sure you're okay?"

"I'm fine. Thank you for coming to see about me."

Calvin nodded. "If you need anything else, you just press that there call button." He pursed his lips disapprovingly as he shouldered his way past Troy.

After Calvin left, Troy turned back to Andrea, shaking his head. "How do you do it?"

"What?"

"Have everyone eating out of your hand like that."

"*You're* not," she said, her gaze meeting his.

Wasn't he? Why else was he here instead of going home when he had the chance if he wasn't falling under her spell, just like everyone else?

"What *are* you doing here?" she asked, as if she'd read his mind.

Good question. He glanced at his watch. "It's still early. I don't suppose you feel like taking a walk?"

"Where to?"

Troy shrugged. "I don't know. There's a coffee shop on this floor. I haven't eaten yet, have you?"

Her blue eyes widened almost imperceptibly. "Are you asking me to dinner?"

"I need to talk to you," he clarified quickly.

"All right." Was it his imagination or did she seem a little disappointed? "Would you mind waiting for me in the hallway? I'll just be a minute."

"Sure." That would give him plenty of time to ask himself just what in hell he thought he was doing.

Troy stepped outside and leaned against the wall. This wouldn't do. It wouldn't do at all. He couldn't afford to screw up again. His involvement with Cassandra Markham had almost cost him everything. What the hell was the matter with him?

He could just hear what his old man would say if he could see his son now. And what about Ray and Mitch? What would they say if they knew their little brother was about to get in over his head one more time? Would they be so quick to try to bail him out this time? Or would they decide to let him sink or swim on his own, just as Gary had done when he'd thrown Troy into the creek behind their grandparents' farm?

Swim, kid! Give it all you got!

Somehow Troy, only three years old at the time, had managed to make it back to the bank, and then he'd lit into ten-year-old Gary with a vengeance. Gary had just laughed, shoved him away like a pesky fly and said, "Now I don't have to worry about you getting yourself drowned when you follow me and my buddies down here.''

Thanks to his brother, Troy had turned out to be the best swimmer of them all and a competitive diver, even getting a full scholarship to the University of Houston. But he wondered what Gary would think if he could see the way Troy was floundering now, and all because a woman who didn't know her own name had caught him completely by surprise.

He sighed, scrubbing his face with his hands. He was a damn fool and he knew it.

After a few minutes, the door opened and Andrea stepped out. She was wearing a blue satin robe over her nightgown and blue quilted slippers. Her hair was pulled back and fastened in a loose braid down her back, making her look incredibly soft and feminine, incredibly desirable.

"I'm sorry," she said. "This is all I have to wear."

"Don't be sorry," he murmured. "You look… beautiful."

His words seemed to catch *her* by surprise. She started to say something, but the light in the hallway ignited the diamonds in her ring as she moved her hand up to smooth back her hair.

Her hand stopped in midair.

The diamonds flashed with cold fire.

And a warning sounded somewhere in Troy's brain. *Back off, you idiot. Back off before someone gets hurt.*

"Uh, the coffee shop's this way," he said, motioning with his hand.

They started down the hallway, each of them careful to keep a distance between them. But as they approached the coffee shop, Troy's arm brushed against hers when he reached out to open the door for her.

A thrill of excitement shot through Andrea. She wondered if she had ever been so aware of a man before. Surely she'd been attracted to her husband. Hadn't he made her heart beat this fast, her knees grow this weak, her stomach flutter like a thousand butterflies had taken flight inside her?

Somehow Andrea didn't think so.

The coffee shop was almost empty. They took a table for two near the windows, and Troy went to get their coffee and a sandwich for himself. While he was gone, Andrea stared out the window at the downtown skyline, picking out the buildings she recognized. It was strange. She knew what the Texas Commerce Tower looked like, could pinpoint the neoclassical lines of the Esperson Building, but she had no idea what her own home looked like or where it was located. She knew she lived in Houston, though. Knew she had been born here. There was no doubt in her mind about that, except...

Something niggled at the corners of her mind. She'd been sent away once, hadn't she? Lived where the winters were long and brutal and the summers much too short. She'd been very unhappy back then, her father dead and her mother—

Abruptly her thoughts cut off, as if a curtain had dropped inside her mind. *Don't think about your mother,* a little voice whispered. *Think about surviving. Think about getting out of here. Think about helping Mayela.*

"Sure you don't want something to eat?" Troy asked as he dropped down in the chair opposite her. He handed her a cup of coffee, then finished unloading his tray.

Andrea shook her head. "No, thanks. I'm not hungry."

"Well, if you're sure." He picked up his ham-and-cheese sandwich and began to eat.

After a few bites, he wiped his mouth with a paper napkin and shoved his plate aside, grimacing. "Hospital food never changes."

"No, I guess it doesn't." She put her coffee cup down, careful to avoid his gaze. "You said you wanted to talk to me."

When he didn't answer, she was forced to glance up. His dark brown eyes studied her with an intensity that took her breath away. Her hands began to tremble, and she clasped them in her lap so he couldn't see.

"What's the matter?" she asked. "Why are you looking at me that way?"

He shook his head slightly. "I can't figure you out."

"What do you mean?"

"Look at you. You're gorgeous, a real head-turner. A face that would be almost impossible to forget, and yet no one has recognized you from your picture. No one's called in about you. No brother or sister, no mother or father. No one."

"Maybe I'm an orphan," Andrea said. "Maybe I don't have parents." As she said it, she knew it was true. She didn't have parents. Not anymore. Somehow she knew her father was dead and her mother was lost to her forever. Andrea felt the sudden heat of tears behind her lids. "Maybe there's no one."

"There must be *someone*," Troy said. "What about your husband?"

"What about him?"

"Why hasn't he come forward?"

Andrea fingered her wedding band. "You said yourself, he may be out of town. Or he may think I'm out of town." That was true, wasn't it? He *could* be out of town....

Yes! She remembered now. The gray-haired man bending down to kiss her on the cheek. It had been a brotherly kiss, completely lacking in passion. *Goodbye, Andrea. I'll see you when I get back. Take care of Mayela for me.*

You know I will. Please don't worry. She'll be safe with me.

A spurt of fear shot through Andrea. She knew as surely as she was sitting there that someone named Mayela was in terrible danger, but Andrea was powerless to help her because she didn't know who Mayela was or where the danger came from.

Andrea thought about telling Troy everything she had remembered, begging him to help her solve this terrifying riddle, but another memory stopped her. Or was it her sense of survival?

I hate you. I want you dead! Dead! Dead! Dead!

She looked down at her robe, almost expecting to see bloodstains covering her hands and spreading over the blue satin of her robe. But her hands were clean, her clothes spotless. The bloodstains were only a memory. But of what?

Andrea's hands began to shake even harder. "I'm tired. I—I think I'll go back to my room."

Troy was watching her carefully, that shadow of suspicion clouding his dark eyes. "We haven't finished our talk."

"There's nothing I can tell you." She pushed herself up from the table. "I don't know anything. I don't remember anything."

Troy stood, too. "Who're you trying to convince, Andrea? Me...or yourself?"

"I know you don't believe me," she said with a desperate edge to her voice. "But I really don't remember what happened. I don't remember anything."

She tried to brush by him, but he snared her arm with his hand. "Then who is Mayela?" he asked, his eyes growing even darker with suspicion.

"Wh-what?"

"You were whispering her name in your sleep. Who is she, Andrea?"

"I don't know."

"I don't believe you." His eyes turned so cold Andrea felt chilled to the bone. "I don't believe you *can't* remember. I think you don't *want* to remember. I think you're *afraid* to remember. What did you do, Andrea? Whose blood was on your dress?"

His hand on her arm sent a thrill of awareness through Andrea, but she kept her expression even. She didn't want him to see how much his touch affected her. "Why don't you just charge me with something if you're so sure I've committed a crime? Why don't you put me in jail and throw away the key?" Despite the bravado of her words, her mind screamed in denial. *Don't lock me in the dark room! Don't leave me by myself!*

As if he'd glimpsed the terror in her eyes, he dropped his hand from her arm. "I'm sorry. I didn't mean to hurt you."

"You didn't hurt me." And he hadn't. Not the way he meant. His grip on her arm hadn't been tight. She could have gotten away from him at any time, but he'd hurt her just the same. Hurt her with his doubts and suspicions.

But who could blame him? If Andrea didn't have doubts about herself, she would have confided in him days ago, wouldn't she? She would have told him about the flashes of memory she was experiencing, about her nameless fear, about the man with the gray hair and the girl named Mayela. She would have told him about the knife...

He lifted his hand and drew his fingers through his hair. "I don't know what came over me," he muttered. "I'm really sorry."

"Forget it. I have." But she hadn't. She would never forget that look of suspicion in his eyes, the accusations. She would never again let herself forget that Sergeant Troy Stoner wasn't a friend, no matter how much she might wish him to be. He was a cop who would do whatever necessary to find out her dark and deadly secrets.

And she would do everything she could to make sure he didn't. Because that was the only way she knew to save herself.

"Come on," he said. "I'll walk you back to your room." He was still looking shaken by what had happened. She suspected his loss of control was out of character for him, and the notion that she was responsible was more than a little frightening.

"Don't bother," she said. "I think it's time we call it a night."

He stopped, gazing down at her. Something flashed in his eyes. Disappointment? Andrea wished she could believe it was so. "Maybe you're right," he said slowly. "Maybe I should have called it a night a long time ago."

And with that, he turned and walked away, leaving Andrea to wonder about this dark and dangerous man who wasn't her husband.

MADISON CAME BY to visit Andrea the next afternoon. It was a strange visit. One minute, Madison was telling Andrea about her mother's cat, which had triggered a memory of a kitten Andrea had had as a child. The next thing Andrea knew, Madison was patting her hand. "Wake up, Andrea."

Andrea opened her eyes and yawned. "What happened?"

"You fell asleep."

"I did?" Panic curled inside her. Andrea moistened her lips. "Did I...talk in my sleep, or anything?"

"No. You were sound asleep." Madison smiled, but her usually open gaze looked a little reserved. "You obviously needed the rest."

"I do feel refreshed," Andrea said. She felt as if she'd just awakened from a full night's sleep, except for the persistent notion that she'd been dreaming about something important. Something revealing. It was like peeking through a piece of cloth. She could see shadows, but nothing concrete. Nothing real.

Her forehead knitted as an image began to clarify.

There he was again, that gray-haired man with the careworn face.

"I can see him," Andrea murmured.

"Who?"

Andrea put out her hand, as if to touch the image. He was looking at her, his eyes shadowed with pain.

An overwhelming sense of sadness came over her. She felt like crying.

"What is it, Andrea? What are you remembering?"

As she continued to watch, the memories unfolded like scenes from a movie. As if in slow motion, the gray-haired man crumpled to the floor. Blood oozed through his fingers where he clasped his chest, and someone screamed, *I hate you! I want you dead!*

A tear rolled down Andrea's face. She felt Madison touch her hand, and she wiped the tear away with her fingertips.

"You remembered something, didn't you?" Madison asked quietly.

"No, it was just—" What? A man dying? A man being murdered? Who had killed him? And why?

I've changed my will, Andrea. When my time comes, you will be well taken care of.

I want you dead. Dead! Dead! Dead!

Andrea's heart thundered in her ears. She looked down at her nightgown, seeing the blood-splattered white dress.

Dear God, what have I done? she wondered frantically. *What have I done?*

"SHE FELL ASLEEP," Madison said.

"Fell asleep? Just like that?" Troy sat across the table from his sister in the hospital cafeteria.

Madison stirred lemon into her tea. "It was really strange, almost as if…"

"What?"

"I don't know. Almost as if she'd fallen into a hypnotic trance."

Troy frowned at his sister. "Did you hypnotize her?"

"No. At least not intentionally."

"Can you do that unintentionally?" His tone was skeptical.

"Not unless there's some sort of trigger that's been implanted in her subconscious that I might have stumbled upon purely by accident."

Troy's frown deepened. "I don't follow."

"Once a patient becomes comfortable with hypnosis, a therapist will sometimes use a word or a phrase, often an image, that triggers instant relaxation. The patient can fall almost immediately into a deep trance."

"You think that's what happened with Andrea?"

"Not necessarily. I'm only speculating. It's curious, though, because the other day when I mentioned hypnosis to her, she seemed frightened by the notion."

Troy sat back in his chair and studied his sister thoughtfully. Something was bothering her. He could tell by the way her dark eyes were having trouble meeting his. "Just tell me one thing," he said. "Do you believe her memory loss is real?"

Madison shrugged. "It doesn't take a brain surgeon to fake amnesia, but honestly? I'm inclined to believe her. I think she may have had flashes of memory, bits and pieces that have come back to her, but Troy…it's what she *can't* remember that worries me. What she won't let herself remember."

Troy nodded. "It worries me, too." It worried him that she had been found wandering down a busy street, with O-positive blood covering her clothing. It worried him that she had a bruise on her arm and a wedding band on her finger, and it worried him that he couldn't seem to get her out of his mind, that he dreamed about her at night and woke up thinking about her each morning.

It worried him that he didn't know what the hell he was going to do about her. His choice should have been clear. In fact, there shouldn't even *be* a choice. She was a married woman. Therefore, no matter what she might or might not have done, she was off-limits to him.

Troy liked to think of himself as an honorable man. A man who didn't go after someone else's wife. But Andrea had gotten under his skin as no other woman ever had.

Not even Cassandra Markham, who had almost gotten him killed.

Just then, Troy saw Tim Seavers walk into the cafeteria, and he raised his hand and motioned him over.

"Pull up a chair," he invited when Tim had walked over to their table.

Tim sat down. "I'm glad I ran into you," he said to Troy. "I've been meaning to call you, but I haven't had a chance. I'm releasing Andrea tomorrow."

"Releasing her?" Madison asked with a note of alarm in her voice. "Where will she go?"

"I don't know. But there's no physical reason for her to remain hospitalized, and we don't have enough beds to keep her any longer than necessary."

Madison turned her dark eyes on Troy. "Where will she go, Troy?"

He shrugged carelessly, but he was wondering the same thing himself. Where *would* she go? She had no money, no credit cards, and she still didn't know her last name. He supposed she could hock her bracelet and wedding ring, but those funds wouldn't last forever. What if her memory never came back?

Not your problem, a little voice warned him. The same little voice that cautioned him each and every time he was about to do something stupid. For all the good it did.

"I have an idea," Madison said.

"I don't like it," Troy said.

"You haven't even heard it yet!"

"I know, but I don't like that gleam in your eyes."

"Don't be ridiculous," Madison scoffed. "My idea is perfectly feasible. Andrea can come stay with me."

"Isn't that violating some sort of doctor-patient thing?" Troy asked skeptically. In truth, he wasn't sure how he felt about Madison's proposal. On the one hand, it would keep Andrea close by, so that he could keep an eye on her. On the other hand, it would keep Andrea close by.

"I'm not her psychiatrist," Madison reasoned. "I'm trying to be her friend. Under the circumstances, I think it's the perfect solution."

"She's right, Troy," Tim said. "Otherwise, where else would she go? I'd hate to think of her living in the shelters."

Madison looked appalled. "You can't send her to a shelter. She wouldn't last a day."

Troy didn't want to think about Andrea in the shelters, either, for any number of reasons, but he had a feeling she was a lot tougher than any of them thought.

"Okay," he said. "I see there's no talking you out of this. I just hope you know what you're doing."

Madison smiled at him in reassurance. "Don't worry about me. Don't worry about Andrea, either. We'll be fine."

But Troy couldn't help worrying. His sister had a habit of picking up strays, and sometimes those strays had a tendency to bite the hand that fed them.

BEFORE GOING HOME that night, Troy decided to swing by the hospital to see how Andrea had taken the news of Madison's proposal. It was late, and the hospital corridors were all but deserted. No one was manning the desk at the nurses' station, and Troy supposed whoever was on duty had been summoned by a patient. He turned the corner and started down the hall when he noticed a doctor wearing green scrubs standing outside Andrea's room. He was pushing open her door with one hand while holding a syringe in the other. It seemed awfully late for a doctor to be paying a call on a patient, and as far as Troy knew, Andrea wasn't receiving any medication.

He called down the hallway. "Tim?"

At the sound of Troy's voice, the doctor's head jerked toward him. Troy was still some distance away. He had only a brief impression of a surgical mask and cap covering most of the face before the doctor whipped around and took off running down the hallway.

"Hey!" Troy bolted after him, but the green-clad figure was already disappearing around a corner. Sliding on the polished tile floor, Troy took the same corner seconds later. A service elevator was located halfway down the next corridor. Just as Troy reached it, the doors slid closed, and the car began to descend.

Pounding the doors in frustration, Troy turned and located the entrance to the stairwell. He slung the metal door back so hard, it bounced off the wall, then slammed with a bang behind him as he charged down the stairs two at a time. Halfway to the bottom, he jumped over the railing to the lower level and continued down six more flights.

There was something ominous about the way the green-clad figure had been lurking outside Andrea's door. Something dangerous about the syringe he held in one hand. Troy had no idea who the figure might have been, but he damn well intended to find out.

Panting hard, his heart beating like a piston inside his chest, he reached the ground floor and slammed open the stairwell door just as the elevator bell sounded outside. Troy raced down the corridor toward the elevators, automatically reaching for his revolver. He got himself into position just a split second before the doors slid open.

There was no one inside.

Chapter Five

Madison's west-side town house was situated in a deeply wooded cul-de-sac a few blocks over from Memorial, in a quiet, elegant part of town. As Madison fished in her bag for the key, Andrea took a moment to look around.

Although the complex was modest in appearance, there was no mistaking the exclusivity of the neighborhood. The postage-stamp front lawns were emerald green and lushly landscaped with crape myrtle, hibiscus and scarlet bougainvillea. No cars were parked along the street. No trash cans lined the walkways. The scene was almost surreal in its tranquillity and a direct contradiction to Andrea's inner turmoil.

She'd talked with Troy earlier that morning before being discharged from the hospital, and he'd told her about seeing someone outside her hospital room last night. Someone dressed in green scrubs and a mask, so that his or her identity was protected. Someone who ran away when Troy called out.

Andrea's heart tumbled inside her as she thought about her first night in the hospital, when she thought someone had been in her room. She'd managed to convince herself her imagination had been playing tricks on her, but now she wasn't so sure.

Who had been lurking outside her door last night? Not a friend, surely. No friend would have tried to visit her so late, hiding his identity. No friend would have run away.

Then who? An enemy? It was staggering to think that someone out there might want to harm her, that someone could actually hate her enough to want her dead. Even though she didn't remember why, Andrea had absolutely no doubt whatsoever that she was in danger. And now so was Madison.

Andrea had been so touched last evening by Madison's invitation to stay with her and so relieved because she really didn't have any place else to go. But now Andrea wasn't so sure they were doing the wise thing. Was it fair to put Madison's life in danger, as well?

But Madison wouldn't take no for an answer, even after Troy had told them about last night. She'd insisted Andrea come home with her, and that was the end of it.

Troy, however, had looked less certain. He, too, had his doubts about this arrangement, and Andrea knew it wasn't just because of the man outside her hospital room last night. Troy still had his doubts about *her*. He still wasn't convinced she was an innocent victim in all this, and truth be told, Andrea couldn't say she was all that sure herself. The images she'd been seeing, the feelings she'd been experiencing—to put it mildly, it was all less than reassuring.

She still didn't know what kind of person she'd been, but she knew one thing about herself. She hadn't told Troy or Madison about the flashes of memory she'd been having, so she knew she was capable of deceit.

What else was she capable of?

Madison finally got the door open, and the two of them stepped into the cool interior of the town house. A tiled

entry led into the large living area, which was light and
airy, done for the most part in peach, cream and teal
green. Several oil paintings hung from the walls, and
when Andrea went to examine them more closely, she
noticed they had all been signed by someone named Beverly Stoner.

"My mother," Madison explained, coming to stand
beside Andrea. They were staring at a scene that seemed
vaguely familiar, a paved courtyard and stone fountain.
The picture seemed so real that Andrea could almost feel
the spray from the water on her face.

"It's very beautiful," she said softly, the beginning of
a memory tugging at the corners of her mind. And then
it burst upon her with the force of a juggernaut. Andrea
stared at the painting as the images rushed through her.

"Do people really live like this? It's like a palace!"

*Someone laughed. A young woman with jet black hair
and onyx eyes. Her voice sounded like music. "Oh, Andrea, you're so much fun! This place is far from being a
palace. It isn't even the biggest house in River Oaks."*

*"But it's so beautiful!" Andrea let her hand trail
through the cool water that splashed from the stone fountain. The spray misted her face, and she closed her eyes.
"I love it here. I wish I never had to leave."*

*"Why would you have to leave? Mayela adores you.
We all do."*

*An almost unbearable sadness came over Andrea be-
cause she knew sooner or later she would have to leave.
She didn't belong in a place like this. She didn't belong
anywhere....*

And then the memories seemed to fast-forward, and
another scene played out in Andrea's mind.

The same fountain splashed in the same lovely courtyard, but a different woman was speaking to her this

time. She, too, had dark hair and black eyes, but she was older, and instead of a soft, lilting voice, her tone was icy with scorn.

"My daughter felt sorry for you, took pity on you. She brought you into her home, treated you like a friend, and look how you repay her. By betraying her memory. You're nothing but a cheap, backstabbing, little gold digger. If Richard thinks I'll stand by and see the two of you married, with my Christina not even cold in the ground—"

Andrea broke off the memory abruptly. She didn't dare take the scene any further, because she had a terrible premonition of what that would do to her. Any illusions she might have had about herself, about the kind of person she had been, would be shattered forever. There would be no deluding herself once the memories returned. No pretending. Just cold, hard reality.

A reality she wasn't sure she was ready to accept.

The burst of memory seemed to have gone on forever, but in actuality lasted only seconds. Madison appeared not to have noticed Andrea's silence. She was still talking about her mother's paintings.

"...often wondered what she might have done with her talent if she hadn't had so many kids to take care of. Then after Gary died, she stopped painting altogether. It's been five years, and as far as I know, she hasn't picked up a brush since." She caught herself then and glanced at Andrea. "Listen to me rambling on like that. You don't even know who I'm talking about, do you? Gary was my brother. He was killed five years ago."

"I'm sorry," Andrea murmured. She had begun to think of Madison Stoner as someone who led a perfect life. She seemed professionally successful, came from a big family and had a past that Andrea doubted very seriously would ever come back to haunt her. But Madison had known grief in her life. She'd known pain, and Andrea realized that nothing was ever as it seemed on the surface. There were always undercurrents, some not so strong, but others so treacherous they would pull you under if you let them.

Those were the undercurrents Andrea worried about. "I'm not sure this was such a good idea after all." She turned to Madison. "Aren't you afraid to have me stay with you? What if that man Troy saw outside my door last night comes looking for me here?"

"Look." Madison tucked her short glossy hair behind her ears. "In the first place, we don't even know if that person was a man or a woman, and in the second place, since he or she was dressed in surgical scrubs, it could very well have been hospital personnel."

"Then why did he run away? Why did he disappear like that when Troy chased him?"

"Maybe *because* Troy chased him. Or her," Madison said. "My brother's not always subtle."

"Still, the person's actions were suspect, you have to admit," Andrea persisted. "And I can't help thinking that if he found me in the hospital, he could just as easily find me here. I don't want you to get hurt because of me."

"You're assuming that the person's intent was to harm you. You don't know that for sure, do you?"

The brown eyes, so like her brother's, studied Andrea intently. Andrea had to remind herself that Madison Stoner, regardless of her kindness and generosity, was a trained psychiatrist, and she was the daughter and sister of cops. Andrea knew it wouldn't be easy fooling her, day in and day out, pretending that her mind was still a complete blank. In spite of the danger lurking outside these walls, there was danger inside, as well. Maybe she would be better off just to leave. Maybe they all would be better off if she simply disappeared.

"Andrea?"

She forced her attention back to Madison. "I'm sorry. What did you say?"

"I said I don't think you have to worry. The complex has a security guard on duty twenty-four hours a day, and no one is allowed through the gates without the access code. My brothers made sure this place was secure before I moved in. You're safe here."

Was she? Was she safe anywhere?

All you have to do is remember, Andrea. Then you'll know where the danger is coming from. You'll know who your enemies are. All of this will finally be over.

But it wouldn't be. Somehow she knew that when her memory returned, the real nightmare would begin.

She rubbed a hand across her forehead, willing away the gnawing doubt that she had done something wrong. Terribly, terribly wrong. Why else did she have these flashes of remorse? This almost overwhelming feeling of guilt?

Why else had she been found covered in someone else's blood?

"You look tired," Madison said. "Why don't I show you to the guest room?"

"No, I'd like to stay out here for a while, if that's okay." She didn't want to be shut away somewhere. She wanted openness, at least the illusion of freedom. She gazed around, admiring the simple yet elegant furnishings. "This room is so soothing."

"I'm glad you think so." Madison smiled and sat down on the couch, curling her feet beneath her. She waved Andrea to the chair facing her. "I like to think of this as my sanctuary, a place where I can get away from all the problems of the world, mine as well as everyone else's."

"But you can't do that with me here, can you?" Andrea's fingers clutched the arms of her chair, but she willed them to relax.

"I don't think of you as a patient," Madison said. "I think of you as a friend, Andrea."

Andrea was touched beyond words. She instinctively knew she didn't make friends that easily, had had maybe one or two really close friends in her whole life. But she'd felt an instant bond with Madison from the first and had to resist the urge to confide in her, to tell her everything she'd remembered. And everything she feared.

Andrea had felt that instant connection with Troy, too, but the bond with him was very different from friendship. What she felt for Troy was an emotion she didn't dare analyze too closely. There was no such thing as love at first sight, was there?

She twisted the ring on her finger, but didn't take it off.

"Can I ask you something, Andrea?"

"Of course."

Madison's gaze was direct, but nonjudgmental. "There's something between you and my brother, isn't there?"

Her insight was terrifying. "No," Andrea said quickly.

Madison sat forward, her dark eyes troubled. "I don't mean to put you on the spot. It's just that...I worry about him."

"Why?"

"This isn't the first time he's been attracted to the

wrong woman." She looked immediately contrite. "I'm sorry. I didn't mean it like that."

Andrea shrugged. "It's all right. I understand what you mean."

"I don't think you do." Madison paused. "You see, several years ago Troy became involved with a woman who almost destroyed him. She was a murder suspect, and he was the detective assigned to the case. She convinced him that she was innocent, and that all she needed was for someone to help her prove it. When Troy tried to help her, she turned everything around, accused him of everything from police misconduct to planting evidence to make her look guilty, and it worked. Her lawyers got her off, but afterward, when Troy confronted her, she went off the deep end, pulled a gun and tried to kill him. It was all a big mess, a terrible scandal, and Troy was suspended pending a formal hearing, which eventually cleared him. But his reputation took a pretty bad beating, and he lost faith in his ability to judge a person's character, both in his professional and personal relationships. He doesn't trust easily, and if he seems a little harsh with you at times, that's why."

"I understand." But in her case, he had good reason not to trust her, Andrea thought sadly. She didn't even trust herself.

"I just thought you should know," Madison said softly. "Troy was hurt very badly once. I wouldn't want to see that happen again."

"I don't want to hurt him." Andrea hoped she didn't sound as defensive to Madison as she did to herself.

"Of course not. But you're married, Andrea. If my brother falls in love with you, someone is going to get hurt."

Fall in love? Why did that notion send such a burst of

excitement spiraling through her? Why did the thought of a man like Troy Stoner falling for someone like her make her want to shout with joy?

Because she was having feelings for him, too, Andrea admitted. She knew, without knowing how she knew, that she'd never felt this way about anyone else. In spite of his doubts and suspicions about her, Troy Stoner was someone very special.

But Madison was right. Andrea couldn't afford to let her feelings get out of hand. Not only because she was a suspect. Not only because she might have done something wrong, and not even because Troy had once been badly hurt.

She couldn't let her feelings for him show because she wasn't free to love him.

A terrible yearning came over her. A part of her knew he was the person for whom she'd been searching all of her life, but she'd found him too late. If she had any decency left inside her at all, she would sever the bond between them, before it was too late.

Before anyone got hurt.

TROY SAT AT HIS DESK, staring at the stack of files in front of him, and decided he wouldn't call his sister to find out how things were going with Andrea, no matter what. By all indications, Andrea was a married woman, and what's more, a suspect. He couldn't afford to let his attraction go any further. Hadn't the past taught him anything?

But his affair with Cassandra Markham had been different. He'd been a lot younger for one thing, and he realized now the fact that she'd been taboo had been the strongest part of her appeal. Troy had always been somewhat of a rebel, and in Cassandra Markham, he'd sensed a kindred spirit that had drawn him as surely as a moth to flame.

It was different with Andrea, although the similarities couldn't be denied. She was a beautiful, desperate woman in a whole peck of trouble. Troy's natural inclination to be the rescuer had been struggling like hell to get out. But it wasn't just that. It wasn't that he sensed a dark and dangerous quality about her, although he did. But after Cassandra, that no longer had the appeal it once did.

No, what he felt for Andrea was something different, something deeper, something harder to define. The fact that she was off-limits to him was not an attraction but a frustration. She was a married woman. What if he got involved with her, and then when her memory returned, she suddenly realized she was deeply in love with her husband? Where would that leave Troy?

Best to stay away from her, he decided, wadding a phone message and tossing it toward the trash can. Best to keep his distance. Because if he didn't stay away, he might start to think that she was attracted to him, too. He might start to wonder if that subtle light that ignited in her eyes when she looked at him was desire. And if that happened—

God help him, if that happened, he might start to forget that she was forbidden.

SHE KNEW she was dreaming but she couldn't make herself wake up. Andrea lay helplessly in the throes of her nightmare, watching the scenes play out before her as if she were looking through the keyhole of a door.

She could see the gray-haired man with the careworn face, the dark-haired young woman with the musical voice, the older woman with the hate-filled eyes and someone else Andrea couldn't quite make out. Someone who stayed in the shadows.

Where was Mayela? She seemed to be the central figure in the drama, but she had yet to take the stage. Was she the one who waited in the wings for her cue? Somehow Andrea didn't think so. The shadow who prowled offstage was a dark figure, an ominous apparition that frightened Andrea, although for all she knew, that lurking presence could have been herself.

Disturbing thought, that.

The young, dark-haired woman with the musical voice said, "Please say you'll stay, Andrea. Your being here has been a godsend for all of us. I don't know what I'd do without you. You're the only one I can talk to. I've been so depressed lately. I've had such terrible thoughts. At times I've actually wondered what it would be like to...do away with myself."

The older, dark-haired woman with the hate-filled eyes said, "My daughter is dead. The police say it was suicide, but I don't think so. I think you had something to do with Christina's death."

The gray-haired man with the careworn face said, "I've changed my will, Andrea. When my time comes, you will be well taken care of."

Suddenly the scene became even more dramatic, but Andrea was no longer watching through the keyhole. The door had opened, and she was there, with the gray-haired man as he clutched his heart and fell to the floor. Blood was everywhere. All over her.

"I hate you! I want you dead!"

An overwhelming sense of guilt washed over Andrea, stronger even than the horror that lay before her. But even as she stood staring at the blood on her hands, a little voice inside her screamed, *Run, Andrea. Find a*

place to hide! If they find you, they'll take you away.
They'll say you've done bad things, terrible things.
They'll lock you in the dark room!

And then a child, a little girl, screamed, "You killed
my daddy! You killed my daddy!"

The focus changed, and Andrea was now watching the
scene through the child's eyes, experiencing the child's
emotions. She thought for a moment she *was* the child,
but then she thought the child must be Mayela. From the
child's eyes, she saw a woman bend over the dead man.
Blood covered her hands as she lifted them in front of
her.

Then Andrea was behind the door once again, observ-
ing both woman and child through the keyhole. The child
was sobbing, screaming in terror. The woman turned her
head toward the sound and smiled, her expression demented.

With deepening horror, Andrea saw that the woman's
face looked like her own.

WHEN ANDREA WOKE UP, she was gasping for breath.
She felt as if someone were choking her, and for a moment, her arms flailed in the air.

But there was no one in the room with her, and as her
heart settled down, the images in her dream began to
come back to her—the gray-haired man, the young, dark-
haired woman, the older woman with the icy voice and
the unseen presence lurking in the shadows. Who were
these people?

The gray-haired man worried her especially because
Andrea knew in her heart he was dead. But *how* did she
know? How could she possibly know, unless...

She got up and walked to the window, staring out
blindly into the darkness. It was all coming back to her,

just as Madison and Dr. Seavers had predicted. Andrea was finding the pieces to her puzzle one by one, and the bigger picture was starting to take shape.

Someone had died, and someone from her dream was the murderer and someone was the victim. But just what role Andrea had played in the grisly tableau was yet to unfold. She wondered how much longer she could prolong the ending.

As long as you have to, said the little voice of survival.

But Andrea was no longer listening to that voice. She was listening to her heart, and it was telling her that the longer she delayed her confession to Troy, the more he would despise her when the truth came out.

Somewhere outside, a shadow moved and Andrea's heart stopped. A tree limb blowing in the breeze, she tried to tell herself, then realized there wasn't a breath of air stirring. The night was still and silent. There was a three-quarter moon, but a lacy filigree of clouds hung over the pale light. Madison's tiny yard lay in darkness. Andrea peered anxiously through the window. Outside, nothing stirred. Nothing moved.

Inside, Andrea's breath was suspended in her throat. Her heart hammered against her chest. He was out there, she thought. Somewhere among the shadows, the figure who had been in her hospital room and the malevolent presence in her dream were waiting. But for what?

For a moment, in spite of her terror, Andrea experienced a brief stirring of hope. If someone was watching her, if someone wanted to harm her, didn't that mean she wasn't the killer? Didn't that mean she was an innocent victim? Couldn't she go to Troy and tell him everything she knew?

But what if he doesn't believe you? whispered the little

voice of reason. *What if he locks you away in the dark room? What would happen to Mayela?*

Who is Mayela? Andrea wanted to scream. Why couldn't she remember her? Why was Mayela in danger, and why was Andrea so sure that she was the only one who could save her?

Andrea couldn't explain it, but the feeling was so strong inside her she was forced to accept it. She had to remain free. She couldn't be sent away. She had to pretend she remembered nothing, because only then could she help the little girl named Mayela.

Chapter Six

By the time Madison got up the next morning, Andrea had fixed them both breakfast. She'd set the table on the tiny patio out back and brought in the paper from the sidewalk. She didn't open the paper, though. She didn't want to see her picture, didn't want to think about the fact that no one had come forward to identify her. Except for that figure outside her hospital room, and the malevolent presence last night.

She suppressed a shiver as she poured freshly squeezed orange juice into two glasses and carried them to the table.

Madison came outside, yawning widely. She gazed at the table in amazement. "This is lovely, Andrea, but I didn't invite you here to be my maid. You didn't have to do this."

"I don't mind. Besides, it's the least I can do." She took a seat across the table from Madison and unfolded her napkin.

Madison took a bite of the scrambled eggs and closed her eyes. "Heavenly! Where did you learn to cook like this?"

From my aunt, Andrea almost said, but then realized

she had no idea who her aunt was, or why she had taught Andrea to cook.

You must be self-reliant in every respect, Andrea. Not only do you need to learn to cook and keep house, but you need a profession. A respectable way to earn a living. Never depend on a man—for either your support or your happiness. Look what happened to your poor mother. If she'd never met your father, she wouldn't be locked up in that awful place today, and I wouldn't have been forced to take in her wayward child. Not that I mind, of course. I've never been one to shirk my responsibilities. But I'm not as young as I used to be, and you can be a handful at times, though I'm sure you always mean well. I just pray you haven't suffered any permanent damage from that horrible ordeal, and you won't suddenly become unhinged one day....

"Andrea?"

Andrea blinked. "I'm sorry. What did you say?"

Madison blotted her lips with her napkin. "Where do you go when you drift off like that?"

"I beg your pardon?"

"You do that a lot," Madison said. "Become completely still and silent. You're remembering something, aren't you?"

"Sometimes," Andrea admitted. "But most of the time it's nothing that makes much sense. Just then, I was remembering something from my childhood. I think I was sent to live with my aunt when I was quite young. She never married. In fact, I think she hated men, and I don't think she had much use for children, either. She was quite happy living alone, and I guess I spoiled her tranquillity."

"That's quite a burden to place on a child's shoulders,

feeling responsible for someone else's unhappiness. How long did you live with her?"

Andrea closed her eyes. "I don't know. A long time, I think. I remember being lonely. We didn't have much company. My aunt didn't like to socialize, and I wasn't allowed to have friends over after school." That same feeling of loneliness came over Andrea now. A terrible sense of isolation. She'd been different from the other kids at school, afraid to get close to anyone, afraid they might find out why she was so different.

"Where are you from, Andrea?"

"Here. I was born in Houston."

"Is that where your aunt lives?"

"No, she lived up north somewhere." Where it was always cold, always winter.

"You said 'lived.' Is she dead?"

That snapped Andrea out of the dreamlike state that had overcome her. She shook her head. "I don't know. That's all I remember."

"Well, that's quite a lot actually." Madison smiled at her across the table. "This is a good sign, Andrea. I don't think it will be long now before everything comes back to you."

Andrea glanced down at the ring on her finger. Sunlight danced on the diamonds. Memories whispered through her mind, and the morning suddenly turned ominous.

Madison said, "There is one thing we should talk about. When you do get your memory back, you should be prepared."

"For what?"

Madison paused, her dark eyes pensive. "Amnesia is a tricky thing. There's still a lot we don't understand about it, but in cases like yours, where there's no apparent physical reason for the memory loss, it seems to be the mind's way of coping with something extraordinarily traumatic.'' She paused again. ''When this event occurred—whatever triggered your memory loss—you weren't able to deal with the shock and so your mind blocked it out, in order to protect you. In your case, this mechanism was fairly extreme because you blocked out everything, not just the actual event.''

''What does that say about me?'' Andrea asked.

''What do you mean?''

''Does that mean I'm...crazy?''

''Of course not. It means you may be a little more adept at self-preservation than the rest of us, that's all. Your mind wasn't taking any chances. It wiped out everything, letting only tiny pieces filter back in until you're ready to cope. It actually makes a lot of sense, when you think about it.''

Andrea glanced up almost fearfully. ''What kind of trauma would cause such a complete block?''

''I don't know, but because of the extent of your amnesia, it almost certainly had to be something extremely stressful. That's what I mean by being prepared. When your memory does return, you'll still have to deal with whatever it was that happened to you.''

''But what if I can't deal with it?'' Andrea asked. What if she'd done something so terrible, so horrible that her mind would never be able to accept the reality? What then? The dark room?

''You're a very strong and determined woman, Andrea, and your instinct for survival is obviously quite strong. I think when the time comes, you'll be able to accept what happened, work through it and go on from there. I have complete faith in you.'' Madison smiled brightly and laid her napkin aside. ''There. Having said all that, I'm going to turn off the psychobabble, as Troy so charmingly refers to my profession, so that we can concentrate on something a little more pleasant. What are your plans for the day?''

It was Sunday, but that meant little to Andrea. She had no memory, which meant she had no past and no future. What kind of plans could she have?

"Because if you don't have any," Madison was saying, "I'd like you to come to dinner at my parents' house. It's a Stoner family tradition, you see, and none of us—not even my brother Ray, the brooding loner of the family, would dare not show up without one whale of a good excuse. And according to my mother, short of being in a body cast, there are no good excuses."

Andrea was on the verge of asking her whether or not Troy would be there. But Madison had said everyone was expected, so obviously that included him. Andrea knew what she should do. She should make up some excuse—surely amnesia ranked right up there with a body cast, didn't it?—and stay home where she would be safe from her emotions.

But Madison was right. The memories were coming back, almost too fast, and Andrea didn't want to be alone with them. She didn't want to have to think about what might have happened, prepare herself for what she might have done.

Besides, she'd been alone so much. All of her life, it seemed. To be asked to Sunday dinner with a family that intrigued her as much as the Stoners was an invitation that was almost irresistible.

If Troy was there, she would avoid him.

If her heart started to pound when she saw him, she would ignore it.

If her stomach knotted when he talked to her, she would pretend calmness.

After all, she'd gotten quite good at pretending, hadn't she?

TROY WAS SITTING in the den, talking to his brother Mitch, when Andrea walked in with Madison. Andrea's silvery gold hair was pulled back and fastened in a loose braid down her back, and she wore a yellow sundress that made her look as cool and tempting as a glass of lemonade on a hot summer's day. The dress bared her shoulders with straps that crisscrossed in the back, and several of the buttons in front had been left undone, so that a tantalizing portion of tanned leg was left exposed.

Beside him, Mitch had been in the process of lifting a beer to his mouth, but the bottle froze in midair. Earl, who had been talking quietly with Ray, let his sentence trail off into dead silence. And Ray, who never showed emotion of any kind, turned his head, and one dark brow lifted slightly when he saw Andrea. Their reactions were registered by Troy only because when he'd first seen Andrea, his heart rate had accelerated so alarmingly, his pulse had jumped so erratically that he'd glanced around at his family to make sure no one had noticed.

He needn't have worried. Every pair of male eyes in the room had vectored in on Andrea and remained there. Even his old man couldn't take his eyes off her, and Troy frowned, experiencing a proprietary emotion that was surely unwarranted.

Everyone stood as Madison made the introductions, and Troy glanced around again, wondering this time what Andrea thought of his family—Mitch in shorts and boat shoes without socks, Ray in faded jeans and a T-shirt, Earl in starched khakis and a long-sleeved plaid shirt and

Troy himself in pleated trousers and a white collarless shirt. Their attire was as diverse as their personalities, but they all had their profession in common. Troy couldn't help thinking that a family of cops had to be a little intimidating to someone like Andrea.

But she didn't look intimidated at all. She looked completely at ease and in control of the situation as she said hello to everyone and stepped forward to shake their hands. Troy thought that both Ray and Mitch held on to Andrea's hand a little longer than was necessary. He moved forward, claiming the spot beside her.

"Sergeant Stoner," she said, an intriguing little glint in her blue eyes. "Nice to see you again."

"It's 'Troy.' I'm off duty today. We all are." She didn't offer her hand to him, Troy noticed, and he couldn't help feeling a little slighted. "I didn't know you were going to be here today," he said, low enough so that he hoped his father and brothers couldn't overhear, though he knew Earl was straining to.

She trained those blue eyes on him. "Madison invited me. I hope you don't mind."

"Why should I mind?" No red-blooded male in his right mind would have an objection to her presence, especially considering the way she looked in that yellow dress, and Troy was no exception. Like his father and brothers, he couldn't take his eyes off her. He vaguely recalled having seen Madison wear that dress before, but it sure as hell hadn't had the same impact.

As if sensing the direction of his thoughts, Madison swept forward and grabbed Andrea's hand. "Come on. I want you to meet my mother."

After the two of them had disappeared into the kitchen, the men all took their seats again. Earl settled back into his recliner, and Mitch turned on the TV. Ray walked over, and the two of them sat on the couch, watching a basketball game. It was an NBA play-off game, and normally Troy would have been just as engrossed, but today basketball was the furthest thing from his mind.

He wandered around the den for a moment, glancing out the window, thumbing through a magazine, then as he walked by Earl's recliner, his father waylaid him.

"That girl with Madison. She's a knockout."

Troy grinned. "I noticed you noticing."

"Man'd have to be dead not to." Earl took a long swig of his beer. "I know all about her amnesia. And about the blood on her clothes."

Troy figured his old man probably knew a hell of a lot more than that. Even in his retirement, Earl was still better informed than any of his sons. After forty years on the force, he had eyes and ears everywhere.

"All right," Troy said in weary resignation. "What do you want to know, Dad?"

Earl stared him right in the eyes. "You behavin' yourself with her?"

Troy couldn't have been more shocked. The question took him completely by surprise, and for a moment, he had no answer. Then he said, "I'm trying to find out who she is, where she's from and where her family is. That's all."

Earl nodded, but there was a glimmer of doubt in his eyes. "Just thought I'd ask." He didn't mention the Cassandra Markham case, but Troy knew that's what his father was thinking about. "Why don't you go on out to the kitchen and see if you can give your mother a hand?"

Troy was glad to escape. He met Madison in the kitchen doorway, and he snatched a chip from the bowl she was carrying out to the den. His mother was at the sink, rinsing vegetables. He walked over and kissed her cheek. "Need some help?"

"Everything's under control, but thanks, anyway. Just stand here and visit with me, okay?"

"That's easy enough." Troy leaned against the counter, watching his mother work. She was a tall woman and still almost as slender as her daughter, with the same short cap of glossy black hair—hers now sprinkled with gray—and the same dark brown eyes. "Where's Andrea?" he asked casually.

"I sent her out to the back porch for some ripe tomatoes." His mother glanced up. "She's such a beautiful young woman, but then, I'm guessing you already noticed that."

"Couldn't help but," he agreed.

"And 'Andrea' is such a lovely name. She told me it was her grandmother's name."

Troy stared at his mother. "She told you that?"

His mother looked up at his tone. "She said she was named after her grandmother. Nothing unusual about that, is there?"

Troy shrugged. "No, I guess not." He paused, then said, "How much has Madison told you about her?"

"Nothing really, except that she has amnesia. Is there something else we need to know?" His mother's dark gaze eyed him curiously.

"I'm just wondering what else she may have remembered that she didn't tell me. I think I need to have a talk with her."

"Troy." His mother turned to him, wiping her hands on a dish towel. "Can't you stop being a cop for one day? She's our guest. Now's not the proper time to interrogate her."

"I wasn't going to do that," Troy said. "I'd just like to ask her a few questions."

"About what?" Andrea was standing in the back door, her arms laden with tomatoes. The red stood out starkly against her pale yellow dress, and Troy was immediately reminded of another dress, covered with blood.

For a split second, their eyes met and no one said anything. Then the kitchen door swung open, and Mitch walked through with Tim Seavers. "Look who the cat dragged in," Mitch said.

Beverly Stoner exclaimed in delight, "Tim! Where in the world have you been keeping yourself!"

In all the confusion, Troy managed to relieve Andrea of the tomatoes, then took her arm and steered her out the back door.

"Where are we going?"

"You haven't seen Mom's garden yet, have you?"

"No. Just from the porch."

They walked down the steps, into the dappled sunlight of the backyard. The air was filled with the scent of roses and the drone of bees. A breeze drifted through the oak trees, stirring the morning glory vines that clung to the trellised sides of his mother's gazebo. The tree house he and his brothers had built a lifetime ago perched precariously on the wide, lower branches on the oak tree.

Andrea laughed delightedly when she saw it, and the sound charmed Troy. Sunlight glistened like gold in her hair, and a tiny yellow butterfly circled her head, as if weaving an invisible halo.

"It must have been wonderful, growing up in a home like this," she said softly. "Having a mother and father like yours, lots of brothers and sisters to play with. You're very lucky."

"Yeah, I guess I am." It wasn't something Troy

thought about much. He'd grown up in this house, surrounded by family, not just brothers and sisters, but aunts and uncles, dozens of cousins. He'd never considered his family anything out of the ordinary, just people sharing a common bond who cared about each other, who watched out for one another. They were like any other family and only extraordinary to someone who'd never had one.

He wondered if Andrea had been an only child, if she'd been lonely growing up. He wondered what her family was like, if she'd ever had anyone to take care of her.

Maybe she didn't need anyone, he thought, but at that moment, he wanted to believe she did. His gaze met hers, and something stirred inside him. Before he could stop himself, Troy reached out to tuck an errant strand of gold behind one delicate ear, and her hand lifted to settle over his. They stood motionless for what seemed like an eternity, her hand capturing his, their eyes meeting and Troy's heart pounding inside him.

What had she done to him? What kind of spell had she cast to enthrall him so completely, to make him forget the hard lessons he'd learned in this life?

What would it take to release him from her spell? A kiss?

Worth a try, he decided, and lowered his lips to hers.

She backed away, dropping her hand from his, and turning to comment on the roses as if nothing had passed between them. As if that brief moment of magic had been conjured by his imagination.

And maybe it had been.

But he had to know. He had to be sure. "Andrea—"

She still wouldn't look at him. "Don't." Not a command but an entreaty, as if she had no strength left to fight him.

He found hope where there should have been none. His heart quickened. "I have to know, Andrea."

"Oh, God." She put her hands to her face. "I've made such a mess of everything, haven't I?"

"What do you mean?"

She shook her head. "It's all so hopeless."

"What is?" He reached for her arm, but she moved away from him again, at last turning to face him.

Her eyes looked bleak, haunted. She held out her hand, and at first he thought she wanted him to take it, but then he saw the flash of diamonds on her finger. "This is my wedding ring," she said.

"I know."

"I have a husband."

"Probably."

"I can't do this, Troy."

"We haven't done anything."

"But I want to," she whispered, squeezing her eyes tightly shut. "Just now, I wanted you to kiss me." It was all Troy could do not to take her in his arms, hold her so tightly she could never get away from him. Never escape him. He wanted to enthrall her, mesmerize her, so that she fell under the same spell she had cast over him.

"Andrea—"

She opened her eyes and looked at him. A calmness came over her features, almost as if a curtain had dropped over her emotions. "Let's not speak of this again," she said. "Let's pretend I never said that."

"You're not asking much, are you?" he said bitterly.

"It's the only way," she said, slipping even farther away. She turned and gazed up at the tree house. "Show me your tree house, Troy," she said a little desperately. "Tell me what it was like to grow up here. Tell me all about your family, everything. I want to hear it all."

The words gushed from her, as if they could somehow erect a safe wall between them. Troy didn't know what to say, what to do, how to feel. He knew she was right. There couldn't be anything between them.

But to know that she felt the same way he did, to realize that she wanted him as much as he wanted her...

It was as if a fist had taken hold of his heart. To have her so close...and not be able to touch her, kiss her, whisper to her all the things he wanted to say to her.

To have found her too late. To know that she could never be his. To realize that when she got her memory back, she would be lost to him forever...

She was already at the bottom of the steps that led up to the tree house, reading a faded sign that had been hammered to the railing years ago: No Girls Allowed (That Means You Madison).

"No girls allowed. What kind of chauvinistic attitude is that?" she challenged.

"A stupid one," Troy said, coming up behind her.

"Then it's okay if I go up?" Andrea glanced back over her shoulder, her eyes twinkling with merriment, as if the last few moments had never taken place.

Troy had no recourse but to do the same. "I won't tell if you won't," he said, brushing past her. "Better let me go first, though. These steps can be pretty tricky. I'll give you a hand up."

She waited until he'd climbed all the way up, then she bounded up the steps, unmindful of her dress, and ignored the hand he held out to her. She hauled herself up to the wooden floor, stood and dusted off her hands.

"Point taken," Troy muttered.

They walked over to the railing and stood staring down at the neighborhood. All the yards and houses were pretty much alike, but the Stoner home still retained a special enchantment for Andrea. Maybe because of the man standing beside her.

"That's the Gilmore house," he said, pointing to the redbrick home behind the Stoner property. "See that window? My brothers and I used to sneak up here at night and watch Lorie Gilmore get ready for bed. I was just a kid, probably not more than seven or eight, too young to know or care what was going on, but I knew it had to be a pretty big damn deal, seeing a girl in her underwear, because of the way Mitch and Gary would carry on."

"What about Ray?"

"Ray was too old for that type of juvenile stuff by then, and besides, he never had to sneak around to get a look at a girl. He always had them falling all over him, the big football jock."

"Did you play football?"

"No. I was a diver."

"You dove off those tall platforms, did all those flips in the air and everything?"

"Yeah, it was great," he said with a grin.

"I'll bet." Especially considering those tiny trunks divers wore. A scene rushed through Andrea's mind, not her memory this time, but her imagination...going wild.

"What was Gary like?" she asked.

"Gary? He was a great guy. The best. He taught me a lot."

"You still miss him."

"We all do. You don't get over something like that. You just get on with your life."

They stood in silence for a moment, each lost in thought, and then Troy said, "You see that house over there?'' He pointed to a white two-story home, half a block away. "When we were kids, a girl named Dana Farrell lived there. The summer he turned fifteen, Gary fell madly in love with her. The two of them were inseparable all through school, and then right before her senior year, her father got transferred to California. She and Gary kept in touch for a long time, but eventually they drifted apart. She went to law school, and Gary became a cop. Years passed, and then one day she got a job in the D.A.'s office down here. She moved back, looked Gary up, and the two of them picked right up where they'd left off in high school. They were engaged to be married when he was killed.''

"I'm sorry," Andrea said, not knowing what else to say. But Troy wasn't telling the story as if he were still grieving, or as if he thought it a tragedy. He was telling it as though he were in awe of their love. As if he couldn't quite understand feelings that ran that deep, that could last that long.

"It's been five years since Gary died," he said. "And Dana's never married. I don't think she's even come close."

"Does she still work in the D.A.'s office?"

"Yeah, she's an A.D.A, an assistant district attorney. In fact, she's supposed to be here today. You'll like her.''

"I'm sure I will."

Silence again. Andrea could feel his eyes on her, but she didn't dare turn to meet his gaze. Didn't dare let him see what was in her own eyes.

"Your turn now," he said softly. "I've told you all about my family—now I'd like to hear about yours."

"But I don't remember my family," she protested. "I don't have anything to talk about."

"You remember your grandmother," he said. "Her name was Andrea."

She did turn to him then. "Your mother told you."

"Why didn't you?"

She shrugged helplessly. "It just came to me when I was talking to your mother. I didn't have time to tell you." But the excuse sounded lame even to her. She turned her gaze back to the yard below them.

"Is Mayela part of your family?"

Andrea's heart skipped a bit. "I don't know."

"You were whispering her name in your sleep that night. You seemed frightened for her."

"Did I?"

"It's an unusual name," he persisted. "Surely you can remember something about her."

She's in danger, and I'm the only one who can save her.

His eyes darkened, and for a moment, Andrea was afraid she'd said the words aloud. Then when she realized she hadn't, she wanted to. She wanted to confess everything to Troy and let him help her. But what if he couldn't help her? What if he didn't believe her? What if they took her away again?

There would be no one to save Mayela. No one to save Andrea, either.

She couldn't say anything, not until she knew what she was up against. Not until she knew she hadn't done anything wrong.

A voice called up to them from the backyard. "Hey, you two! You'd better get down here fast or Bev says she's going to put you in charge of the cleanup detail!"

Andrea stared down at the young woman in the yard. She wore a denim skirt and a white tank top that showed off a gorgeous tan. Her hair was light brown, thick and straight and cut bluntly at her shoulders. She waved when she saw they were looking down at her.

Troy waved back. "That's Dana," he said. "Come on. I want you to meet her."

Andrea climbed down the steps behind him, relieved that for the moment at least, she had been given a reprieve.

Chapter Seven

On Monday morning, Troy was at his desk, going through the stack of case files Lucas had given to him last week, when the lieutenant came out of his office and walked over to Troy's cubicle.

"Looks like you're about to get a break, Stoner."

Troy glanced up. "Yeah? On which case?"

"Jane Doe, the one with amnesia."

Troy's heart slammed into his chest. "What kind of break?"

"There's a woman in my office claims to know her."

Troy's head snapped toward Lucas's office. Through the glass partition, he could see a woman seated across from Lucas's desk. "Who is she?"

"Name's Claudia Bennett. *Dr.* Bennett. She's a psychiatrist."

A chill of foreboding came over Troy. "A *psychiatrist?*"

"Yeah. Says Jane Doe's a patient of hers. Thought you might want to talk to her."

He sure as hell did. Troy stood, shoving back his chair with more force than was necessary. It hit a filing cabinet with a loud bang, and Lucas raised a brow. "Sorry,"

Troy mumbled, grabbing his notebook and pen and heading toward the office.

The woman looked up when Troy walked in. She didn't stand, didn't smile and didn't offer Troy her hand when he introduced himself.

He took a seat behind the lieutenant's desk and studied her for a moment. She looked to be in her late forties, conservatively dressed in a navy blue suit, white starched blouse and low-heeled pumps. There was an exotic quality about her, but Troy couldn't pinpoint her ethnicity. Her eyes were tilted at the corners, but they were light, not dark, and her black hair was pulled back into a severe French twist that gave her face a tight, almost masklike appearance.

The impression was further enhanced by the thick makeup she wore, which was several shades lighter than the skin on her hands, making Troy wonder if she was deliberately trying to obscure her origins. Rather than giving her a striking appearance, however, the pale skin and blue eyes against her thick black hair made her look even more foreign. Almost alien.

Troy thought her one of the most intimidating-looking women he'd ever met.

"You say you recognize the woman in this picture?" He held up the photograph of Andrea that had run in the newspaper and on TV.

Dr. Bennett nodded. "Yes. She's a patient of mine. Her name is Andrea Malone."

Malone. The name was like an electrical jolt through Troy. Already Andrea was slipping away from him. Now she had a complete name, a whole identity. A life that didn't include him.

"How long have you known her?"

"Several months."

"Her picture first ran in the papers and on the news four days ago. Why has it taken you so long to come forward?"

Dr. Bennett shrugged. "I've been out of town, on business. I just returned last night, and this morning, when I saw Andrea's picture in the paper, I came straight here. Is she in trouble?"

"She's not under arrest, if that's what you mean."

"I'd like to see her."

"I'm sure that can be arranged," Troy said. "But first there're a few questions I need you to answer for me."

Something flashed in her eyes, a mild annoyance that was quickly stifled. "What is it you wish to know?"

"I need to know about her family, where she lives, if there's someone who can take care of her while she recovers."

"Are you telling me that no one else has come forward to identify her? I'm the first?" Although her tone sounded astonished, her eyes remained calm. Almost too calm, in Troy's estimation.

"Can you tell me about her family?"

"Of course. As I said, her name is Andrea Malone, and she lives in River Oaks with her husband, Richard, and his daughter, Mayela."

Mayela. Troy recognized the name instantly. So Mayela was Andrea's stepdaughter. And Richard Malone was her husband.

"I think there's also a mother-in-law who resides at the estate, and perhaps a brother, but I'm not quite sure," Dr. Bennett was saying. "And as for having someone to take care of her, Andrea has a veritable army of servants who are at her beck and call. Richard is…quite wealthy."

Troy made note of the fact that Dr. Bennett referred to Andrea's husband by his first name. He wasn't sure what it meant, but it did seem a little unusual. Then again, maybe not. Maybe he was looking for some reason not to believe the woman. Not to trust her.

"You told Lieutenant Lucas that Andrea is a patient of yours."

"That's correct." She glanced at her watch. "Look, I really didn't come down here expecting an inquisition. I'm a busy woman, Sergeant, and I really don't have time for this. If you'll just tell me where I can find Andrea..."

"It's not quite that simple."

"Why not?" A look of alarm flashed in the woman's eyes. "You said she's not in any trouble."

"I said she isn't under arrest."

Dr. Bennett blinked. "Well, I just assumed..."

"There are some questions that have arisen as a result of Andrea's...condition, and I'm hoping you can answer them for me."

"Such as?"

"Where is her husband? Why hasn't he come forward to identify her?"

"I can't speak for him, of course, but he could be out of town. Richard travels extensively. He's seldom home. He may not know about Andrea. And then, of course, it could be because..." Her voice trailed away.

"Because?"

Her blue eyes drilled him. "Andrea is my patient. I cannot violate her confidence. But it's no secret that she and Richard have had their difficulties."

Troy felt a queasiness somewhere in the pit of his stomach, as if he were invading Andrea's privacy, eavesdropping on the most intimate details of her life, but he had no choice. He had to find out just what the hell was going on, whose blood had been on her clothing when she'd been picked up.

"What kind of difficulties?"

Dr. Bennett shifted ever so slightly in her chair. "Richard is a great deal older than Andrea. There are certain problems inherent in that kind of relationship."

"How much older?"

"I'd say at least twenty years."

Troy wondered how he felt about that revelation. At the moment, he was too numb to react to much of anything. Later, when he had time to think, to digest everything Dr. Bennett was telling him...

"Dr. Bennett, are you suggesting the reason Andrea's husband hasn't come forward is because they may have had a fight?"

"If she'd left him, he might not know she was missing, would he?"

"That doesn't explain why he hasn't seen her picture in the paper or on the news."

Dr. Bennett shrugged. "Like I said, Richard travels extensively. He may be out of town, as I was."

"And there's no one else in this city who could have recognized her?"

"I don't believe Andrea has lived in Houston all that long. She'd only recently moved here when she got the job as nanny to Richard's daughter."

Nanny? Andrea was a nanny? Somehow that didn't surprise Troy as much as it might have. In spite of her defensiveness at times, her keen instinct for survival, there was a gentle quality about Andrea that would naturally attract children.

"How did she come to marry her employer?" he mused, more to himself than to Dr. Bennett.

"Richard's first wife died," she said, "not long after Andrea came to live with them. It was all very tragic. The little girl, Mayela, was devastated." Dr. Bennett glanced at her watch again. "I really do have other appointments."

"Just a couple more questions. You said it was no secret that Andrea and Richard were having problems. Is that why she was seeing you?"

"No." A shadow crept over the woman's features, a subtle darkening that sent another chill through Troy. "Andrea's problems were much more serious than that, but I'm not at liberty to discuss them with you or anyone else."

ON THE WAY TO MADISON'S town house, Troy called his sister and asked her to meet him there. He told her briefly about Dr. Bennett, about the information she'd supplied concerning Andrea and that he was going over to tell her what he'd learned. Dr. Bennett was following him in her car, so that if Andrea agreed, the doctor would be able to talk with her immediately. Dr. Bennett had insisted.

Andrea answered the door wearing a light pink T-shirt and denim overall shorts that must have come from Madison's closet. Her eyes lit with pleasure when she first saw him, then she quickly masked her emotions by gazing past him at the dark car that pulled to the curb behind his.

"Who is that?" she asked.

Troy glanced over his shoulder. The windows in the BMW were tinted so darkly that Dr. Bennett was obscured behind the wheel. But he knew that she was there, watching Andrea closely, perhaps trying to evaluate her from a distance.

He turned back to Andrea. "Let's go inside."

Although he tried to keep his tone even, he saw fear leap to her eyes. She cast another anxious glance at the black car as she stepped back for him to enter. Then she followed him into the living room.

"What's wrong?" she asked before he could say anything.

"Maybe we'd better sit down."

"I don't like the sound of this," she said, but she did as he suggested.

Troy, however, remained standing. He went to the window and peered out. Dr. Bennett had gotten out of the car and was standing by her door. She wore dark glasses, but Troy knew she was gazing at the house, at him.

He turned away from the window. "Your name is Andrea Malone."

He heard the sharp intake of her breath. "How did you find out?"

"Someone identified your picture from the paper."

"Who?"

"A woman named Claudia Bennett. She's a psychiatrist."

"Oh, God." It was hardly more than a whisper, but Andrea's words seemed to echo through the room. Her face drained of color, and her eyes suddenly looked hollow. The reaction was strong, and Troy couldn't help but wonder why.

"She says you're a patient of hers," he said carefully.

Andrea didn't say anything this time, but he could see her fingers gripping the arms of her chair. "What else did she say?"

"You have a husband named Richard."

No reaction this time, and Troy thought that odd. There was not even so much as a flash of memory or a glimmer of recognition in her eyes when he mentioned her husband.

"You have a stepdaughter named Mayela."

"*Mayela.*" Her gaze shot up to connect with his.

"Yes. At least that's one mystery solved."

"Is she all right? Is she safe?"

Troy frowned. "I don't know. I haven't had a chance to contact your family yet, but why wouldn't she be?"

"No reason. I...just wondered."

It was more than that, but Troy didn't press. "Dr. Bennett is here," he said. "She wants to talk to you."

"*Why?*"

"To make sure you're the woman she thinks you are." Troy realized his phrasing was a little strange, but he didn't know how else to say it. "Will you see her?"

"I don't know." Andrea got up and walked to the window, parting the blinds to stare out. "Is that her?"

"Yes."

Andrea glanced at him over her shoulder, her expression bordering on desperation. "Why do I have a psychiatrist, Troy?"

He'd been wondering that very thing himself, almost as desperately, but he forced himself to shrug casually. "Lots of people see psychiatrists for a lot of different reasons."

"But not me. I wouldn't, unless..."

"Unless what?"

"Unless I was scared." She turned back to the window.

"Scared of what?"

She didn't answer him. Instead, she said, "I don't recognize her. She doesn't look familiar to me."

"Maybe when you talk to her, it'll come back to you."

"Maybe I don't want it to." She faced him. "Maybe I don't want to remember."

His heart bounced against his chest at the look in her eyes. "Why not?"

"You *know* why not," she almost whispered. "Troy—"

He put his arms around her and pulled her against him, closing his eyes as he pressed her head against his shoulder and buried his face in her hair. She smelled so good, felt so right...

But it wasn't right. Today he'd learned without a shadow of a doubt that Andrea had a husband. He'd learned the man's name, and soon he'd have a face to put with that name.

But until then...

Until that time, he could almost pretend that Andrea was his. That nothing else mattered except the way they felt about each other.

As if reading his thoughts, she stiffened in his arms, and for a moment, Troy thought she was going to pull away. But instead, she lifted her face, and his lips touched hers, a whisper-soft kiss that burned all the way to his soul. Just for a moment, just for a heartbeat, she kissed him back, and then she did pull away.

"I can't do this," she whispered.

"I know."

"It isn't right."

"I *know.*"

"Troy, I'm sorry—"

"It's all right. My eyes have been wide open from the moment I first met you. Don't blame yourself." *You play with fire, you have to expect to get burned,* he thought bitterly. He ran a hand through his dark hair and looked away.

"She's still out there," Andrea murmured.

Troy glanced back to find that she was staring out the window. "She's not going away, Andrea."

"I have to talk to her, don't I?"

"Sooner or later."

"I guess it might as well be now." She turned back to him, her expression bleak. "The sooner we find out...everything, the better off we'll all be." But her words lacked conviction.

DR. BENNETT FRIGHTENED Andrea. It wasn't just the conservative way she was dressed or the reserved way in which she greeted Andrea. It wasn't even the way she observed Andrea as if she were a specimen under a microscope. What frightened Andrea the most was the knowledge Dr. Bennett possessed about her. The secrets that might have been revealed in their therapy sessions.

Dr. Bennett turned to Troy and said briskly, "Is there somewhere Andrea and I can speak in private?"

"I'll step outside," Troy said. "Take all the time you need."

Andrea wanted to scream at him, *No! Don't leave me alone with her! I'm afraid. So very afraid...* But then she told herself she was being ridiculous. She had obviously trusted Dr. Bennett enough at one time to go into therapy with her. Surely the woman only meant to help her.

Besides, Andrea could no longer rely on Troy. She had a husband, a man named Richard Malone.

She was Mrs. Richard Malone.

Andrea glanced up to find Troy watching her, as if he knew everything she was thinking. An overwhelming sense of guilt came over her. *What have I done?* she thought. So many people had been hurt. Because of her?

Andrea had the horrible premonition she was about to find out.

When the door closed behind Troy, she glanced uncertainly at Dr. Bennett. The woman smiled, but there wasn't the slightest bit of warmth in her eyes. "Shall we sit?"

Like an automaton, Andrea took a seat. She clasped her fingers in her lap, but said nothing.

Dr. Bennett crossed her legs and studied Andrea confidently. "What's this I hear about amnesia, Andrea?"

An odd question, surely. Andrea said, "Didn't Sergeant Stoner tell you? I've lost my memory. I don't remember anything about my life."

"You don't even remember Richard, your husband?"

Andrea shook her head.

Dr. Bennett leaned forward. "Do you remember the last time we talked, Andrea?"

"No. I don't remember you at all."

"Shall I tell you why you were seeing me?"

Andrea nodded, but she wasn't at all sure she wanted to know.

"This isn't the first time you've had an abnormal loss of memory."

Andrea looked at the woman in shock. "What—what do you mean?"

"Much of your childhood has been blocked from your memory. I suspect something violent happened to you in the past."

Andrea's insides were quaking with fear. The woman's words had a disturbing ring of truth about them. "That's why I was seeing you?"

"Partly. And partly because of the nightmares."

"What...nightmares?"

Dr. Bennett glanced away. "You were having dreams about killing your husband."

The woman's words were shattering. Andrea felt their impact as if they were physical blows. "No."

"It's imperative that we continue your therapy," Dr. Bennett said with a note of urgency in her voice. "We have to find the root of those nightmares. We have to find out what you're blocking from your past. If we don't..." Her words trailed off ominously, and Andrea felt sick. The implication was clear: if they didn't find out what was causing her problems, there was no telling what she might do.

She got up and walked to the window to stare out at Troy. Madison had just pulled into the driveway, and the two of them were leaning against her car, deep in conversation. As if he could feel the force of her stare, Troy turned his head, so that he was looking at the window where Andrea stood. Their eyes met, and with an effort, Andrea let the blind snap back into place.

Dr. Bennett stood. "I'm sure you're anxious to be reunited with your family, Andrea, but once everything's settled, we need to talk again. The sooner the better." Her smile was still without warmth. She gathered up her purse, and strode across the room to the front door, pausing with her hand on the knob. "I'm glad I found you, Andrea. You have no idea how worried I've been about you."

Then she opened the door and stepped out.

"DR. CLAUDIA BENNETT, this is Dr. Madison Stoner, my sister."

"Dr. Bennett," Madison said warmly, offering a hand that the older woman seemed reluctant to accept. "Your reputation precedes you. I read your book, *Dark Journey*, in college. It was a primary factor in my decision to become a psychiatrist.''

Something flashed in the blue eyes, something Troy couldn't quite define. Dr. Bennett tried to smile, but the action seemed more of a grimace. ''I'm flattered. Am I to assume you've been treating Andrea?''

''Not really,'' Madison said. ''I've talked with her, but I've tried to be more of a friend to her than anything else.''

''I take it she's staying in your home?'' Dr. Bennett asked with open disapproval.

''She had nowhere else to go,'' Madison explained. ''It was either here or a shelter. I think you would agree this arrangement is the more preferable of the two.''

''I don't know that I would agree with that altogether,'' Dr. Bennett said sternly. ''This arrangement is most unorthodox.''

''Normally I would agree with you, but every situation is different, every patient unique. I don't think I've done Andrea any harm by giving her a place to stay.'' Madison was obviously about to get her dander up, and when that happened, God help anyone who got in her way. Troy decided he'd better run interference.

''Look,'' he said, ''the important thing here is that now we know her name. We can locate her family and find out what the hell is going on.''

Dr. Bennett gave him a withering look, barely hiding her contempt. ''I'm sure you're right, Sergeant Stoner. Perhaps the best thing would be for Andrea to come with me now. I can take her home, talk with her family and make sure she is not put under any more undo stress.''

Troy glanced at Madison, who was shaking her head

behind Dr. Bennett's back. Her eyes told him in no un-
certain terms that Andrea would not be going anywhere,
at least not yet, and perhaps for the first time in their
lives, brother and sister were in complete agreement.

Troy said, "Before Andrea goes anywhere with anyone, *I* need to talk to her family."

"Why?"

"Because there's still an ongoing investigation."

"Into what?"

"I'm not at liberty to discuss the details," Troy said,
taking some satisfaction in the irritation that flashed
across the woman's face.

She turned to Madison. "I'd like to discuss my patient
with you," she said. "May I call your office tomorrow?"

"Please do." Madison extracted a card from her purse
and handed it to Dr. Bennett.

Dr. Bennett glanced at the card, then put it in her bag.
"I trust we'll be speaking again, Sergeant Stoner."

"I'm sure we will," he agreed, but it was a prospect
he didn't look forward to.

ANDREA STOOD by the window when Troy and Madison
entered the room. She didn't look at them, didn't move
a muscle, and her stillness reminded Troy of that first
night when he'd seen her in the emergency room. Had
that really only been a week ago?

Madison said, "Andrea, are you okay?"

"Yes, I'm fine," she said without turning.

Madison glanced at Troy. "I'll go make some iced
tea."

When she'd exited the room, Troy walked over to
stand beside Andrea at the window. For a long moment,
neither of them said anything. Then Andrea took a deep,

shuddering breath, and said very softly, "I have a husband. His name is Richard Malone."

"I know," Troy said, because there didn't seem to be anything else *to* say.

Chapter Eight

The house in River Oaks was startling in its whiteness, and more imposing than Troy had expected. It was a home built to impress, faintly reminiscent of a style he'd seen in the Caribbean, but more formal with two distinct wings and a colonnaded front entrance.

A uniformed maid answered the door, and Troy showed her his badge and ID. "I'm here to see Richard Malone."

"Mr. Malone is out of town."

"Do you know where I can reach him?"

She shook her head. "I don't know his schedule."

"Who would know?"

"His secretary, I guess. Maybe Mrs. Andropoulos."

"Mrs. Andropoulos?"

"Mr. Malone's mother-in-law."

Andrea's mother? For some reason, Troy had assumed Andrea's parents were dead. "Does Mrs. Andropoulos live here?" When the maid nodded, he said, "Is she home? I'd like to speak with her."

The maid hesitated, casting a quick glance over her shoulder.

Troy said, "It's important. Tell her it's in regard to Andrea."

The woman's gaze snapped back to his. Silently she stepped aside so he could enter, then led him into a spacious living room with a wall of windows that looked out on a lush courtyard and fountain. She told him to wait while she announced him to Mrs. Andropoulos, then turned on her heel and exited the room.

Troy looked around, admiring the almost stark but artistic furnishings. A circular marble stair with a mahogany rail rose to a second-floor bridge that connected the east and west wings, and it was on this bridge a few moments later that he saw a woman staring down at him.

His initial thought was that she looked vaguely familiar, although he knew at once she wasn't Andrea's mother. As she slowly descended the stairs toward him, the familiarity faded, and he realized that she was older than he'd first thought, probably close to fifty. But she was still a handsome woman—tall, slender, with a regal bearing that suited the dark purple silk dress and heavy gold jewelry she wore.

Her hair was thick and black, hanging past her shoulders, and her olive complexion was flawless, her cheekbones high and elegant, her eyes dark and piercing. She had the look and manner of a woman who worked hard to retain her youthful appearance, but the fight wasn't an easy one and the bitter signs of defeat were beginning to tell around her eyes and her mouth.

She didn't smile as she entered the room, regarding him coldly as she crossed the marble floor toward him. "I'm Dorian Andropoulos. Estelle tells me you're here about Andrea."

"That's right."

"What has she done?"

Troy glanced at her in surprise. "Why do you think she's done something?"

Dorian walked over to the mantel and extracted a slender cigarette from a porcelain box, then took her time lighting up. She regarded him through a cloud of blue smoke. "You're a police detective, aren't you? I assume you're here because Andrea is in some sort of trouble."

"Not the kind of trouble you mean," Troy said. "But she does have a problem."

"What kind of problem?" Dorian elevated her chin so that she appeared to be looking down at him.

"She has amnesia."

One dark brow shot up. "*Amnesia?* You mean…she doesn't remember anything?"

"Not much. Nothing that has told us why she was wandering down a busy street in the middle of a thunderstorm."

"Wandering down… What on earth are you talking about?"

"Andrea was found walking down Westheimer a week ago Sunday night, completely disoriented. A patrol officer picked her up and took her to the hospital."

"Is she still in the hospital?"

"No. She's staying with a friend."

A frown flickered between Dorian's brows. "What friend?"

"We'll get to that in a moment, but first I'd like to ask you a few questions."

The frown deepened. "What kind of questions?"

"Did you see Andrea that Sunday night?"

"I was out with friends most of the day. I didn't get home until quite late."

"So you didn't see her that night?"

Dorian flicked him a glance. "I believe that's what I said."

"You have no idea what happened to her?"

"None whatsoever."

Troy paced the room, taking in the elegant surroundings, the expensive furnishings. For some reason, it was hard to picture Andrea in this room, but maybe that was because he didn't *want* to picture her here. Didn't want to consider that she might actually belong here.

But even as the thought settled in his mind, his eyes lit on a framed picture on the baby grand piano near the windows. He walked over and picked it up.

Andrea—wearing a white suit, her hair dotted with tiny white flowers—smiled up at him. The man beside her wore a somber dark suit, white shirt, conservative striped tie. Judging by his gray hair and the deep crevices around his mouth and eyes, he was at least twenty years older than Andrea. He, too, smiled for the camera, but there was a look of sadness in his eyes, a weariness in his features.

Troy turned, still holding the picture. "Is this Richard Malone?"

Dorian's lips thinned. "Their wedding photograph."

"I'd like to borrow this."

She suppressed a shudder. "Take it, by all means."

Troy resisted the urge to look back down at the picture, to stare at Andrea's beautiful face. Instead, he studied Dorian Andropoulos. "Can you tell me how to get in touch with Mr. Malone?"

"You can't. He's leading a team of his top executives on a camping trip through the Rocky Mountains. One of those survival-training missions that are supposed to promote teamwork and leadership. There's no way to reach him."

Great, Troy thought. *Just great.* Another missing piece to an already frustrating puzzle. "What's the name of his company?"

"Malone International. It's a consulting firm."

Troy took out his notebook and pen to jot down the information. "Do you know when he'll be back?"

"Not until next week, I'm afraid."

"You haven't heard from him since he left?"

"No," Dorian said. "But as I understand it, that's the whole point of those kinds of trips. To be completely incommunicado with the rest of the world so that one must rely solely on one's wits."

"When did he leave?"

Something flickered in Dorian's eyes, an emotion Troy couldn't define. "Actually he left a week ago Sunday. He had a late flight to Denver that night, where he was to meet up with the rest of his group."

Troy tried not to react to her revelation. "Do you know if he drove himself to the airport?"

"As I've already told you, I was out all day. Richard was gone when I got home. His car is missing, so I assume it's at the airport."

"What time was his flight?"

Dorian shrugged. "Around ten, I believe."

"Do you know if Andrea was home at all that night? If she and Richard spoke before he left?"

"I'm afraid they're the only ones who can answer that question for you. The maid is off on Sundays, and May-ela, my granddaughter, was spending the night with a friend that night. If anyone *was* here with Richard before he left for the airport, it had to be Andrea."

"Does she have her own car?"

"A white Jaguar."

"Is it still here?"

"Yes, as a matter of fact."

"You didn't think it odd that she'd been gone for days and her car was still here?"

Dorian shrugged. "I suppose I just didn't give it much thought."

"Didn't give it much thought? Mrs. Andropoulos, Andrea's been gone for over a week. Why did no one in this house bother to report her missing?"

"No one reported her missing," Dorian said coldly, "because no one missed her. This isn't the first time she's disappeared, but just like a bad penny, she always turns back up."

The woman's malice toward Andrea was a troubling thing. Once again, Troy tried to picture Andrea in this house, but the image was too incongruous. "Are you telling me you didn't see her picture in the newspaper or on TV?"

"I don't watch television and I rarely read the newspapers. The stories are just too depressing."

An answer for everything, Troy thought grimly. "What kind of car does Richard drive?"

"A Mercedes."

"Does Andrea ever drive his car?"

"Sometimes."

"Is it possible she may have driven Richard to the airport in his car?"

Dorian gave him an odd, probing look. "That would be easy enough to find out, wouldn't it? Couldn't you just check to see if Richard's car is at the airport?"

That was exactly what he intended to do. But Troy wished he could end the investigation here and now, before he found Richard Malone's car, before he found out anything else about Andrea and Richard and that Sunday night. He was beginning to get a sick feeling in the pit of his stomach. "Mrs. Andropoulos, when Andrea was found, her clothes were covered with blood that turned out not to be hers. Do you have any idea whose blood it might have been?''

Dorian gazed at him in shock. ''My God. So she *is* in trouble. I've been so worried something like this might happen—''

''Something like what?'' Troy observed her closely. She appeared to be shocked by what he had told her, but something about her eyes, those cold, dark eyes, made him wonder. He had a feeling Dorian Andropoulos was a woman with her own secrets.

She watched smoke curl from her cigarette. ''Nothing. It's just…I've never trusted that woman.''

''But the maid said you're Richard's mother-in-law. Wouldn't that make you—?''

''I am *not* her mother,'' Dorian said through clenched teeth. Her dark eyes narrowed into twin slits of anger, and her mouth thinned. The fading beauty Troy glimpsed earlier all but vanished.

''What exactly is your relationship to Andrea?''

''We have no relationship. Richard's first wife, Christina, was my daughter.''

''I see.'' Obviously this was a sore subject with Dorian. ''How did Andrea happen to become the second Mrs. Malone?''

A furious drag on her cigarette, another cloud of smoke, and then she tapped ashes into a crystal ashtray with a bloodred fingernail. ''Andrea worked for my daughter. She was my granddaughter's nanny. I warned Christina not to hire her, but she wouldn't listen to me. Andrea had never worked as a nanny before, came with no recommendations except for a friend of Christina's, hardly more than an acquaintance really, who had met Andrea through her son. Andrea was the boy's teacher at a private school here in Houston. The friend knew Christina was looking for a nanny, and she introduced her to Andrea. Christina was immediately taken with her.''

Troy knew how that could happen. Andrea had charmed everyone in the hospital, including his own sister. Including *him.* She had a way about her. She made people want to help her. Maybe it wasn't a deliberate manipulation—he hoped not a manipulation at all—but the ability was there nonetheless.

"My daughter was going through a difficult time," Dorian continued. "She suffered from severe depression, and the problem worsened after Andrea moved into this house."

"Were you living here then?"

The barest hint of resentment flashed in Dorian's eyes. "Not then, no. I came to help take care of my granddaughter after Christina died."

"But wasn't Andrea still her nanny?"

"Oh, yes." Dorian stubbed out her cigarette. "You couldn't have pried that woman out of this house. She knew what she wanted from the first, and she didn't rest until she got it. Poor Richard was so distraught over Christina's death that he didn't see it coming. Never knew what hit him."

"How did your daughter die, Mrs. Andropoulos?"

Those red nails toyed with another cigarette. "She committed suicide."

Troy made a mental note to check the records when he got back to the station. "How long have Andrea and Richard been married?"

"Not long. Barely a month."

Just a month, Troy thought. If he'd met Andrea five weeks ago, would it have made a difference? Could he have persuaded her to change her mind and *not* marry Richard Malone? He wanted to believe he could have, but as Troy gazed around the magnificent home, he had to ask himself how the hell a cop could ever compete with this.

He glanced back at Dorian. "How soon after your daughter's death did Andrea and Richard begin seeing each other?"

"Almost immediately. They were married almost six months to the day Christina was buried. When I heard the news, I couldn't believe it. I went to Richard and begged him to reconsider. How much did we really know about Andrea Evans? I asked. How much could we trust her? I was worried about Richard and frightened for my granddaughter."

"Frightened?"

Dorian looked up, her cool gaze measuring. There was no trace of grief, no hint of any emotion except anger in those piercing black eyes. "The police ruled my daughter's death a suicide, but I never believed it. I always thought—"

"Telling tales out of school, are we, Dorian?"

The cultured, masculine voice spoke from the entranceway, and both Dorian and Troy turned toward the sound. The man standing in the doorway was tall and slender, well dressed and well-groomed. *Fine tuned,* Troy's mother would say.

"Robert, this is Sergeant Stoner with the police department," Dorian said.

The man's brows lifted in surprise. "Robert Malone," he said, walking over to shake hands with Troy.

"He's here about Andrea," Dorian said.

"Andrea? What about her?"

"It seems she has amnesia," Dorian said. "According to Sergeant Stoner, she was found a week ago Sunday night with blood all over her clothing."

Robert's gaze shot to Troy. "My God, was she in an accident? What happened? Is she going to be all right?"

"She wasn't physically harmed," Troy said.

Robert frowned. "Then I don't understand. If she wasn't hurt, why does she have amnesia?"

"Her doctors believe she may have witnessed something traumatic."

"Like what?"

"I was hoping someone here could tell me," Troy said. "Where were you that night, Mr. Malone?"

"Let me think." Robert was still trying to act casual, but there was a definite look of alarm in his eyes. "Oh, yes. Now I remember. I drove over to Louisiana to do some gambling for a few days."

"Anyone with you?"

"I always have better luck when I gamble alone."

Dorian looked on the verge of saying something, then decided to keep her mouth shut. She lit up her second cigarette and exhaled a thick haze of smoke. "Aren't you going to ask about the blood, Robert?"

A look of annoyance flickered across his features. "You said she wasn't hurt."

"That's right," Troy said. "The blood on her clothing wasn't hers."

"Then whose blood was it?"

"That's what I'm trying to find out."

Robert shook his head. "I don't understand any of this."

"What's to understand?" Dorian said. "Obviously our little Andrea has gotten herself into some big trouble. Right, Sergeant?"

"Not necessarily. Andrea hasn't been charged with a crime. She's free to come and go as she pleases."

Dorian looked startled. "But what about the blood?"

"What about it?"

"You can't just let her get away with it."

"Get away with what, Mrs. Andropoulos? Do you have evidence that a crime was committed? Can you lead me to a body or to a murder weapon?"

"Of course not."

"Then you see my problem." Troy picked up Andrea's wedding picture from the piano, and turned toward the door. "As I said, Andrea is not being held, so I assume now that she knows where she lives, she'll return home as soon as possible." He glanced at Dorian, then at Robert, who had walked over to the bar and poured himself a drink. "Is there any reason why she shouldn't?"

Robert didn't say anything, but he knocked back the splash of vodka in his glass, then turned to replenish it at the bar. Dorian looked as if she'd like to do the same.

"I'll be in touch, then," Troy said. At the doorway, he paused and glanced back again. "By the way, do either of you happen to know Richard's blood type?"

"Why, yes," Robert said, swirling the vodka in his glass. "It's the same as mine, as a matter of fact. O-positive."

Chapter Nine

Before going over to Madison's, Troy swung by the station to check his messages. He riffled through the slips of paper while he put in a call to Malone International. But after waiting on hold for five minutes, then getting the runaround for another ten, he finally hung up, frustrated. According to the staff at Malone International, there was no way to get in touch with their CEO. That much Dorian Andropoulos hadn't lied about.

But how much else of what she had told him could he trust? Especially the things she'd said about Andrea. Dorian had gone out of her way to paint Andrea in the most unflattering light possible—a gold digger who had conned her wealthy employer into marrying her while he was still grieving for his first wife.

And what about Dorian's inference that Andrea might have had something to do with Christina Malone's death? *The police ruled my daughter's death a suicide, but I never believed it. I always thought*— There had been little doubt what she would have said—or at least implied—if Robert Malone hadn't interrupted them.

Troy tried to analyze the information he'd heard at the Malone mansion without bias, but the truth of the matter was, he didn't want to believe any of it. He didn't want to believe that Andrea had had anything to do with anyone's death, or that she had married a wealthy older man for his money.

Troy didn't want to believe her capable of such deviousness, and yet there was definitely a dark side to Andrea. Secrets were hidden inside her. When those secrets were revealed, would Troy still be able to convince himself that Andrea Malone was an innocent woman?

He thought about Cassandra Markham and everything he'd done to convince himself of *her* innocence. He'd wanted to believe in her until the bitter end, and look where that had gotten him.

Sighing heavily, he picked up the computer printouts on his desk and began to pore over the latest lists of missing persons and homicides that Leanne Manning, the department's computer expert, had sent over earlier.

Lieutenant Lucas, coffee cup in hand, came out of his office a few minutes later. He'd been headed for the coffeepot, but when he saw Troy, he veered over to his desk.

"We must have had close to half a dozen calls this morning," he said. "Seems everyone in the city suddenly recognizes Andrea Malone's picture."

Troy glanced up. "Makes you wonder why it took so long, doesn't it?"

Lucas shrugged. He set his empty cup on Troy's desk. "Not really. People don't pay much attention to that kind of thing. I've always suspected those pictures on milk cartons are a big waste of time."

Troy figured that was probably sad but true.

"What'd you find out about the family?" Lucas asked.

"A weird bunch," Troy said. "Her husband's out of town, no one seems to know how to reach him and his former mother-in-law and his brother seem to be pretty well dug in at the mansion. They weren't upset by Andrea's disappearance, and they sure as hell weren't overly anxious to get her back."

Lucas leaned against Troy's desk and crossed his arms. "You talked to Andrea yet?"

"Not yet. I'm heading over there in a few minutes, but I had a few things to check out here first. I've gone over the missing-persons and homicide reports every day since Sunday week, but I haven't been able to find one single thing to connect her with anyone on the lists. Two homicides had the same blood type, but both had eyewitnesses to the crimes and the suspects are already in custody."

"What are you checking, Harris County? Maybe you need to widen the search."

"I doubt it. According to the lab, the blood on her dress was still fairly fresh when Dermott picked her up that night. I don't think she'd gotten very far from whatever the hell it was that happened when he saw her. It's possible she could have been running away from the mansion."

"You think she whacked somebody at the house, then fled on foot?"

Troy shrugged. "No one's missing except her husband, and according to his office, he's away on business." Troy wondered why he didn't mention Richard Malone's blood type, and the fact that it matched the blood found on Andrea's dress. "I keep thinking about the sedative found in her blood. Why would she take a sleeping pill if she was planning to kill someone?"

"Maybe it wasn't planned," Lucas said. "You know as well as I do that drugs affect people in different ways."

"Her doctor said this drug is harmless."

"Doctors have been known to be wrong," Lucas said. "I'll feel a lot better once we locate Richard Malone. Have airport security look for his car, and if they don't find it, put out an APB. Sooner or later, he has to turn up."

Yeah, but in what condition? Troy wondered. The sick feeling he'd gotten at the mansion hadn't gone away when he'd left. Instead, it was getting worse all the time, and he couldn't shake the premonition that Andrea was headed for trouble. Big trouble.

Lucas pushed himself off the desk and picked up his cup. "Keep me posted, Stoner."

"Will do."

Troy cleaned up his desk as best he could, then dropped by Records on his way out. Leanne was there, sitting hunched over her computer terminal, scowling at the information scrolling across her screen. She looked up and grinned. "Hey, Stoner, any luck with your Jane Doe?"

"Some. I know who she is now and where she lives, just don't know whose blood was on her clothes. Or how it got there."

"I sent over the latest missing-persons and homicide reports," she told him.

"Yeah, I got them. Nothing so far, but keep giving me the updates, okay? Meanwhile, I'd like you to run a list of names through the system for me. Anything comes up on any of them, you give me a call."

He handed Leanne a piece of paper, and she glanced at the list of names. "I'll see what I can find out, but it could take a while."

"No problem. Just let me know if anything turns up."

After signing out the Christina Malone file, Troy

walked out of the building, automatically slipping on his sunglasses. His efforts were a long shot, and he knew it. If the computer turned up anything useful on the names he'd given to Leanne, he'd be surprised. But there was nothing else he could do right now. Nothing else to go on. No body, no weapon, no evidence of a crime except for the blood.

He got into his car, turned the ignition, then shifted into gear and drove out of the parking lot. His mind churned with everything he'd learned that day. The whole setup at the Malone mansion worried him. He didn't like Dorian Andropoulos and he didn't trust Robert Malone. Sending Andrea home to them would feel a little like sending the Christians to the lions, but what choice did he have? Andrea belonged with her family, and there wasn't a damn thing Troy could do about it.

The sooner he accepted that, the better off they'd both be.

ANDREA STARED at the picture of herself and a man Troy said was Richard Malone, and a deep sense of foreboding stole over her. She felt weak, dizzy with terror as she stared down at the gray-haired man with the careworn face. There was no question now. She knew without a doubt who he was.

He was the man she had seen murdered in her dreams.

The image of blood was so strong in her mind that Andrea gasped, dropping the picture to the tile floor in Madison's kitchen. The glass in the frame cracked, and when Andrea bent to pick it up, she nicked her finger on the edge. A drop of blood fell on Richard's face, and the symbolism was almost unbearable.

Troy took the picture from her. "You've cut yourself.'' Though his tone was gentle, his gaze was dark and—Andrea thought—accusing.

"It's nothing," she murmured.

"Here." Madison took charge. She drew Andrea over to the sink, turned on the faucet and doused the finger in cold water. Andrea cringed but didn't pull away. The pain gave her something else to focus on, gave her a moment or two to pull herself together before she had to face Troy again.

Madison wrapped a towel around Andrea's finger. "Just keep applying pressure. The cut isn't deep. The bleeding should stop in a minute."

"I'm fine," Andrea mumbled. Troy was watching her when she turned from the sink. He still held her wedding picture, and Andrea's heart plunged to her stomach when she saw the look on his face.

He knows, she thought.

Somehow Troy knew about the memories and the dreams she'd been having. He suspected more was going on than she was telling him. That was why he seemed so cold and remote.

So unreachable.

Andrea's heart filled with bitter regret.

"Why don't we all sit down?" Madison suggested. She led the way to the tiny breakfast alcove, where a white wicker dinette had been placed in front of a bay window.

Andrea took her seat and clasped her trembling hands in her lap. Across the table, Troy couldn't seem to take his eyes off her. Andrea didn't think she'd ever been so aware of someone staring at her, studying her. What did he see when he looked at her? What did he think? What did he feel?

Did he still want her, after today?

"Don't you want to know about your family?" he asked softly.

"Of course." *No!* She didn't want to know. She wanted to go on pretending she didn't have a family. She wanted to just keep thinking about Troy, dreaming about how it might be if—

"I met a woman named Dorian Andropoulos. Does that name ring a bell?"

Reality came crashing in. A vague uneasiness crept over Andrea. She couldn't place the woman's face, but she knew she'd heard her voice. *You're nothing but a backstabbing, little gold digger."*

Andrea shuddered. "Who is she?"

"She says she's your husband's mother-in-law. His first wife's mother."

Andrea glanced up. "She…lives with us?" It was the first time she'd referred to herself and Richard as an *us,* a couple.

Troy's mouth tightened. "Apparently. So does your brother-in-law, Robert Malone. Do you remember him?"

Andrea searched her mind, but she had no recall of a brother-in-law. No masculine image came to her at all except for the gray-haired man with the careworn face. Richard Malone. Her husband.

She took a deep breath. "What did you find out about me?"

"Quite a lot, actually." Troy's expression remained neutral, but something flickered in his eyes. "Your name before you married was Andrea Evans."

Andrea tried not to react, but a shudder wracked her. *You know about the little Evans girl, don't you? It was so tragic….*

Her gaze darted away from Troy, as if he somehow might be able to read her thoughts by gazing into her eyes. "What else?"

For the next several minutes, Troy recounted to Andrea and Madison everything he'd learned at the Malone mansion. At least, he said it was everything, but Andrea suspected he was holding something back from her.

She listened in horrified fascination as he described Dorian's animosity and Robert's cool detachment, how neither of them had reported her missing because they hadn't missed her. Not only did her family not want her back, but it sounded as though they might actually hate her. Why? What had she done that was so terrible? What kind of person had she been?

Apparently the kind who made a lot of enemies.

The kind who married a wealthy, grieving widower six months after his first wife died.

The kind of woman who could be married to one man and deeply attracted to another.

"I don't think I like what I'm hearing," she murmured. "Could I really have been so bad?"

Something in her tone must have gotten to Troy, because he reached across the table and took her hand. Andrea did lift her gaze then, and their eyes met. And suddenly she forgot all about Madison, sitting at the table with them, and about Richard, a husband she didn't even know. She forgot everything except the way Troy was looking at her.

Something stirred inside her, a longing so deep and so powerful, Andrea felt her breath quicken. She wished they were alone and she was free. She wished she and Troy were the only two people in the world right now.

But they weren't.

And no amount of wishing would change the terrible truth.

Troy said, "Look. I wouldn't put too much stock in what Dorian Andropoulos had to say. She's obviously a very bitter woman. I doubt there are too many people she does like."

Madison, who had been sitting quietly until now, cleared her throat, as if to remind them of her presence, and said, "He's right, Andrea. Don't judge yourself by what someone else says about you. Especially someone who may have a personal bias. You know what's in your heart. You know you're a good person. That's all that matters."

But Andrea didn't know she was a good person. That was the trouble. If she were a good person, why did this awful feeling of guilt come over her at times? Why would she feel so much remorse if she hadn't done anything wrong? But what? What had she done? And what did it have to do with Richard Malone?

Was he really out of town? Andrea didn't think so, and for a moment, she toyed with the notion of telling Troy what she'd seen in her dreams, what she had remembered. She thought of confessing to him that she was almost certain Richard was dead, murdered, but how could she? How could she tell Troy she thought her husband was dead when she might very well be his murderer?

She was the logical suspect, wasn't she? She'd been found with blood on her clothing. According to Dorian Andropoulos, Andrea had married Richard for his money. She was a cold, devious woman capable of anything. What further proof would Troy need?

Andrea remembered just enough to point the finger at

herself, but nothing at all that would help clear her. She couldn't tell Troy. If he didn't believe her—and maybe even if he did—he'd have no choice but to arrest her. She would be locked away somewhere with no way to prove her innocence, no way to defend herself against Dorian's allegations and no way to protect Mayela.

It all came back to the child, although Andrea still hadn't figured out why. She just *knew*. Mayela needed her, and Andrea had to get home to her. Now.

She lifted her gaze to meet Troy's. "When can I go home?"

Something that Andrea wanted to believe was regret flashed in his eyes, but he shrugged, as if her words meant nothing to him. "Whenever you want. I'll drive you there myself."

"She took it pretty well," Troy said. "Better than I expected."

Madison looked at him in disbelief. "What are you talking about? She was terrified. Didn't you see the way her hands were shaking? She was an emotional wreck."

"She seemed calm enough to me." Too calm and too damn anxious to get back home.

Well, what had he thought? That she would chuck it all, the mansion in River Oaks, the wealthy husband, the expensive clothes and jewelry and say, *I don't want to go back. I'll divorce my husband, leave my family, forget I was ever rich. Those things mean nothing to me anyway.*

Obviously they *did* mean something to her. She couldn't wait to get back to them.

Troy didn't like the bitterness that suddenly rose like a dark cloud inside him, but he couldn't help it. He got up and walked across the room, staring blindly out the window over the sink.

"Troy," Madison said softly. "You knew she had a family. A husband."

"Yeah, I knew."

"I hate to see you this way."

He shrugged. "I'm a big boy. I can take it."

She got up and walked over to him, placing her hand on his shoulder. "Maybe you should talk to her, tell her how you feel."

"You know I can't do that. Besides..." He paused. "She already knows."

"And?"

"And nothing." Troy turned to her, his expression bleak. "If she felt something for me once, it's obviously gone now. She's starting to remember her past. Her husband. Did you see her face when she looked at his picture? Maybe she even remembers that she loved him."

"But you don't sound too convinced of that."

He ran his hand through his hair. "It was a weird setup over there, Madison. Tell me what the hell Malone's first wife's mother is doing living with them in the first place? And that leech of a brother..." Troy glanced at Madison. "I'm worried about her going back there."

"What do you mean?"

"Those people are cold. Cold and greedy."

Madison frowned. "You don't actually think they'd try to hurt Andrea, do you?"

Troy's fears had been nameless until now, but he realized that was exactly what he was afraid of. "Remember the way she was found. Wandering down a busy street at night. Blood all over her clothing."

"Yes, but that blood wasn't hers."

"I know." The blood was O-positive, the same as Richard Malone's. "But what about the guy I saw outside her hospital room the night before you brought her here? I keep thinking about the way he held that needle. I keep thinking about the way he ran away. He meant to harm her, Madison."

"You can't know that for sure. You said he was dressed in hospital scrubs and that his face was covered with a surgical mask. In fact, you said you couldn't tell if it was a man or a woman."

"That's true. For all I know, it could have been Dorian Andropoulos."

"You don't really believe that."

"I don't know if I do or not." He gave Madison a hard look. "You didn't see her. You didn't talk to her. There's not much I'd put past her."

"So what are you going to do?"

He shrugged. "What can I do? You heard Andrea. She wants to go home."

"But if you told her your suspicions—"

"I can't do that. I don't have anything but a gut feeling that something is wrong in that house, and lately I'm not too sure I can trust my own instincts. But I tell you what I *can* do." His features settled into grim lines of determination. "I'm going to keep digging until I get to the bottom of all this. I'm not going to let it rest."

"I didn't think you would."

"The first thing I have to do is find Malone."

"And when you do find him, what then?" Madison asked. "What if he's exactly where he's supposed to be? What if there's never an explanation for the blood on Andrea's clothing? Will you be able to let it go then? If you find her husband, will you be able to walk away from her?''

More questions, Troy thought. More questions he couldn't answer. ''I don't know,'' he said honestly. ''I just know that neither of us can go on like this.''

Chapter Ten

Andrea stared up at the mansion, trying to experience some sense of relief, some feeling of coming home, but all she felt was a deep uneasiness. She didn't belong here. This wasn't her home. How could she be married to a man she didn't even remember?

Not exactly true, she reminded herself. She did have memories of Richard Malone. Memories she wished she *could* forget.

She glanced at Troy as he pulled the car in front of the mansion and stopped. His mouth was set in a harsh line, and his eyes looked hard and unreadable. Andrea shivered, feeling his remoteness.

"Are you ready?" he asked, his tone devoid of any emotion.

"I guess so."

Ever since he'd brought her news of her family earlier, Troy had made an obvious effort to withdraw from her, and Andrea had no choice but to do the same. She was home now, and she couldn't afford to be distracted. She had to protect Mayela from whatever darkness lurked within that house, and Andrea's feelings for Troy—and his for her—couldn't be allowed to matter.

But as he leaned over and opened her door, his arm

brushed against her breasts, and a spasm of desire shot through her. As if he'd felt the shock himself, Troy turned, so that their eyes met. Their lips were only inches apart, and Andrea's breath caught in her throat.

She wanted him to kiss her. Wanted it more than she could remember ever wanting anything in her life. Just one kiss. One last expression of the love they didn't dare admit before she walked into that house and into her past.

Before she could stop herself, Andrea lifted her hand to caress his face. He closed his eyes, as if her touch were almost unbearable, and then he turned his head, so that his lips skimmed along her palm.

And still Andrea could not breathe. Still she could not make herself open that door and get out. Still she could not quite admit that Troy Stoner would never be hers. Could never be hers.

He took her hand and kissed each finger, his mouth warm and urgent against her skin. He gazed down at her, his eyes dark and clear and incredibly sexy as he whispered her name on a hot breath of desire.

Andrea trembled. If he kissed her, she wouldn't be able to resist. If he held her, she wouldn't be able to pull away. If he made love to her, she could easily forget that she had married Richard Malone, and that he might be dead at this very moment.

"Oh, God," she whispered.

"You don't have to go in there," Troy said. His eyes grew dark and urgent. "You don't have to go inside that house, Andrea." He stopped short of asking her to go away with him, but Andrea knew that's what he meant, what he wanted.

She drew a ragged breath, his appeal almost too powerful to resist. But even as the temptation almost overcame her will, the front door of the mansion opened, and

Andrea could see a woman in a uniform standing at the top of the stairs. A little girl in a bright red dress appeared at the woman's side.

Andrea couldn't take her eyes off the child. She looked to be about seven, with long black hair and a solemn expression that made her seem older. When the little girl saw Andrea sitting in Troy's car, she shot past the maid and flew down the stairs toward them.

Andrea got out of the car. An overwhelming sense of love swept over her. Without thinking, without analyzing her reaction, she opened her arms, and the child rushed into them. Andrea embraced her, lifted her, and the little girl's arms crept around Andrea's neck, holding her as if she would never let her go. "I knew you'd come back! I knew it!"

"Mayela," Andrea whispered, stroking the child's thick curls. "My little May."

Over the top of Mayela's head, Andrea saw Troy. He'd gotten out of the car and walked around, so that he was standing not two feet away from them. He had to have seen Andrea's unbridled response to the child. He had to have heard her call the child by her nickname. Her actions were hardly those of a woman who couldn't remember her past, but neither were they the actions of a cold-blooded murderer, were they?

Could she feel this much love for a child whose father she had killed?

She put the child down, but Mayela clung to her hand. "Dorian said you weren't coming back, but I knew you would. I just knew it."

"Of course I came back," Andrea said, her response automatic. She was aware of Troy's gaze on her. "I couldn't leave you, could I? Aren't we best friends?"

"Yes, but—" The child's expression grew serious

again. Her blue eyes, so striking against all that dark hair, looked troubled as she gazed up at Andrea. "Dorian said you don't remember me."

Andrea knelt beside Mayela and gently placed her hands on the little girl's shoulders. "I've been...sick, May, and I'm not quite well yet. But I'm getting better, and even if I don't remember specific things about you, I still remember how special you are and how much I love you. I could never forget that."

The child looked appeased, but only for a moment. "Do you remember Daddy?"

You killed my daddy! You killed my daddy!

The child's tortured scream drove through Andrea with the force of a lightning bolt. She gasped, putting her hand to her heart as Mayela's face blurred before her. Andrea couldn't distinguish the child's features anymore. Couldn't see the dark hair or the troubled blue eyes, but she could still hear her screams. She could still feel the child's terror.

Andrea stood and backed away from the child. Dimly she was aware of Troy's hands on her arms, steadying her. "Easy, now," he murmured.

His voice brought her back. For a moment, Andrea leaned against him, drinking in his warmth and strength and comfort. Then she saw Mayela's face. The child looked as if she were about to burst into tears.

"I'm sorry," Andrea whispered. She was still too stunned by the force of the memory to do much more than stare down at the child in regret.

Troy said, "Andrea's still not well, Mayela. I've brought her here so you can take good care of her. Will you do that?"

Mayela nodded. Hesitantly she approached Andrea and took her hand. "Don't worry, Andrea. I'll bring you ice cream and read to you and draw pictures for you, just like you do when I'm sick.''

Andrea's throat tightened with emotion. Somehow she knew that Mayela was the first person who had truly cared about her in a long, long time. Ever since Andrea was a little girl and her own daddy had—

Had what? Died? Why was it she could remember that her father loved her, but she couldn't remember what he looked like? Couldn't remember how or when he had died?

But he *was* dead. She knew it just as surely as she knew Richard Malone was dead.

She looked down at Mayela with a sudden rush of despair. The child didn't know yet. No one knew yet except Andrea. And that could only mean—

She started to panic again, started to withdraw from Mayela, but Andrea forced herself to remain calm. She didn't know what had happened to Richard. She didn't know for sure he was dead. She couldn't know. Maybe he *was* out of town. Maybe he would come back and the three of them would be a real family.

But Andrea knew they'd never been a real family, just as she knew she'd never been in love with him. She couldn't feel the way she did about Troy if she had ever loved her husband.

That begged the question, of course, of why she had married him. But as Andrea looked up at the imposing facade of the mansion, she wondered if that answer was all too evident.

She glanced back at Troy. He had stepped away when Mayela had taken her hand, as if purposefully distancing himself from them. He said now, ''Do you want me to go in with you?''

Andrea shook her head. "That won't be necessary. I know you have to get back."

It wasn't what she'd wanted to say, but Andrea knew it was time to sever the ties, tenuous as they were, that bound them together. Until and unless she could come to him free of and unencumbered by her past and by her deeds, she had to let Troy go.

He stared at her for a moment longer, then turned and got in his car. A wave of emotion washed over Andrea as she watched him drive away, and she had to blink back her tears.

"Who is that man?" Mayela asked. She clung to Andrea's hand.

"He's a policeman, but he's also a friend." Andrea's eyes were still on the spot where Troy's car had disappeared down the street. She couldn't look away.

"He helped you?" the child wanted to know.

"Yes, he did."

"Then he's my friend, too."

Andrea tore her gaze away from the street and smiled down at Mayela. Then, with a deep breath, she turned and looked up at the house. "I guess we should go in."

Mayela's small hand squeezed Andrea's fingers. "Don't worry," she said. "I'll take good care of you."

DORIAN ANDROPOULOS and Robert Malone proved to be every bit as daunting as Troy had warned her. They were both waiting for her in the large living room that opened up just past the stairs. As Mayela led Andrea inside, she held steadfastly to Andrea's hand—not because of her own fear, Andrea thought, but because the child was trying to protect her.

Against what? Andrea wondered with a shiver.

The question was answered the moment she set eyes

on Dorian. The woman's expression, her whole demeanor exuded hostility, and the chill deepened inside Andrea's heart.

The man seated on the sofa, legs crossed, arm draped over the back in an almost studied pose of casualness, bore a striking resemblance to the man in the picture Troy had shown her. But Richard Malone—both in the picture and in her dreams—wore a mantle of strength and character that this man would never be able to achieve. Though he was smiling at her, there was a kind of covert deviousness in his eyes that was almost more chilling than Dorian's open animosity.

As if sensing her unease, Mayela tightened her grip on Andrea's hand. Across the room, Dorian's gaze narrowed on them both. Her elbow was propped on the arm of a chair, and a cigarette smoldered between two fingers. "So," she said, "I see you two have found each other again. Welcome home, Andrea."

There wasn't a drop of warmth in her tone.

"Thank you," Andrea murmured.

Robert got to his feet. "Shall I fix you a drink? A little vodka always hits the spot after an especially trying ordeal."

Trying ordeal? Was that what she was going through? Andrea thought it an understatement. She declined his offer. "No, thanks. I don't drink."

Robert's brows soared. "So you remember that, do you?"

"Just how much do you remember?" Dorian asked. She, too, got to her feet, so that she was no longer having to look up at Andrea.

Andrea shrugged. "Not much, really. I have flashes of memory, more like impressions, I guess you'd say."

"Well," Robert said, turning with drink in hand.

"This is all very fascinating. Do you have any idea how you came to be suffering from this…problem?"

"The doctor said it appears to be psychosomatic," she explained. "I must have seen something or…heard something that was extremely traumatic."

"Do you have any idea what it was?" Dorian's dark gaze swept over Andrea, as if assessing what other damage might have been done to her. Then her eyes lit on Mayela, and her gaze sharpened. "Mayela," she said, "go upstairs to your room."

"But I want to stay with Andrea."

Dorian stamped out her cigarette. "Do as you're told. This is an adult conversation, and you have no business being here."

Though what she said might very well be true, her words were too harshly spoken. Andrea felt the little girl stiffen in defiance. "I won't! You can't make me! You're not my mother! Andrea is my mother now. Daddy said so."

"Mayela!" Dorian turned on Andrea. "This is your doing. She never would have spoken to me like that before you came here. Christina would not have tolerated such behavior."

Christina hated you, Andrea thought with a flash of memory, but she held her tongue. She knelt beside Mayela. "She's right. You shouldn't speak to your grandmother that way. I think you'd better apologize."

Mayela folded her arms and clamped her lips together stubbornly, but only for a moment. Then a spice of mischief twinkled in her blue eyes. She turned to Dorian. "I'm sorry, *Grandmother,*" she said sweetly, drawing out the last word.

Though Andrea couldn't fault the child's tone, she instinctively knew something was wrong. She glanced up to find Dorian's face contorted with rage. "Go to your room at once," she ordered through clenched teeth.

This time Mayela must have known she'd pushed too many of Dorian's buttons, for she whirled without argument and dashed out of the room, pausing only briefly at the bottom of the stairs to call over her shoulder, "Things are going to be different around here now that Andrea's home! You wait and see!"

Andrea wished she could share the child's confidence, but at the moment, she felt vastly overwhelmed.

Robert finished his drink and poured himself another. "Let's get back to this traumatic thing that may have happened to you," he said. "What could it have been?"

"I wish I knew," Andrea said, although she didn't. That was the last thing she wanted.

The doorbell sounded, but neither Dorian nor Robert made a move to answer it. Andrea rose instinctively, then remembered that the Malones had a maid to perform such trivial tasks.

Was she used to being pampered? Andrea wondered. She doubted it. Troy had told her she and Richard had only been married a short time, and before that, she had been Mayela's nanny. One of the servants. Was that why she felt so out of place in this house? Was that why Dorian and Robert seemed to resent her so much?

Shivering, Andrea moved to the glass doors that led out to a walled courtyard with a fountain. The setting looked familiar to her, and she thought about the painting in Madison's living room that had elicited such a strong memory. Was this the courtyard and fountain she had remembered? She closed her eyes, and an image came to her.

Christina was standing by the fountain, her eyes dark with despair. "I don't know what's wrong with me, An-

drea. I can't seem to snap out of this depression. Richard is gone so much. He's never here, and when he is, all he thinks about is his company. He hardly knows our daughter, and I...well, I'm afraid I haven't been much of a mother to her lately. I don't know what we'd do without you. You've been so good for Mayela. She loves you so. Promise me you'll always take care of her, Andrea. Promise me you'll never leave her.''

The memory shattered as a masculine voice spoke from behind her. Andrea turned to see a man stride into the living area. "What the devil is going on, Dorian? Some cop's been calling the office looking for Richard—'' His voice broke off as his gaze lit on Andrea. "Andrea. You're back.''

He'd been heading for Dorian, but now he changed course, quickly crossing the distance to Andrea. He had his back to Dorian and Robert as he put his hands on Andrea's arms and bent to kiss her cheek. His fingers slid over her skin, almost stroking her, and the intimacy shocked her.

She backed away, searching her mind for some scrap of recognition, but the man was a complete stranger to her. He was tall, with the lean, athletic build and the bronzed skin of a man who played tennis several times a week at the club. His hair was brown streaked with gold, and his eyes were a clear, probing gray. He was dressed as elegantly as Robert Malone, but where Robert's appearance was almost a study in fastidiousness, this man wore his expensive clothing with the carelessness of someone who possessed supreme self-confidence. He was handsome and he knew it.

He frowned down at her. "What's wrong? Why are you looking at me like that?''

Andrea tried to answer him, but no words came out.

She stared at his mouth and suddenly remembered how his lips had felt against hers.

Sometime, somewhere, this man had kissed her.

What's more, he was looking at her as if he might do so again.

Who in God's name was he?

Andrea took another step away from him. "Who are you? How do I know you?" she asked a little desperately.

His frown deepened. "What are you talking about?"

"Haven't you heard?" Dorian asked, walking toward them. She came over and linked her arm through his. "Andrea has amnesia. The police didn't tell you?"

"I didn't talk to the police. My secretary said some detective, a sergeant something-or-other, was trying to locate Richard." He turned to Dorian. "What the hell is going on?"

She shrugged. "No one seems to know. Andrea was picked up by the police a week ago Sunday night. Her clothes were covered in blood. But no one, including Andrea, seems to know whose blood it was. Or why she can't remember."

"My God," the man said, gazing at Andrea in fascination. "No wonder you seem so frightened." He looked as if he might make a move toward her again, but Dorian's grip tightened on his arm. "Amnesia," he said. "You mean you don't remember anything?"

"Not much," Andrea said.

"You don't...remember me?" His tone was incredulous, his eyes deep and probing. He made Andrea very nervous.

She moistened her lips. "I'm afraid not."

"This is Paul Bellamy," Dorian said. "Richard's business partner. He was the best man at your wedding."

Something flashed in the man's eyes, a look of anger.

Andrea said, "I'm sorry, but I still don't remember you."

He nodded, but his expression told her he didn't believe her. She couldn't have forgotten him.

Dear God, Andrea thought. What kind of relationship did she have with this man? Why could she remember his kiss so vividly?

He'd been the best man at her wedding, Dorian said. Maybe he'd kissed her then. Kissing the bride was a tradition, wasn't it?

But the kiss Andrea remembered hadn't been a chaste peck on the cheek. She could remember him holding her so tightly she could scarcely breathe as his tongue invaded her mouth. She'd felt...what? Excited? Aroused?

No, panicked, Andrea thought suddenly. He'd frightened her with that kiss.

They all frightened her. The walls of the house began to close in on her. She could hear the voices of Richard and Christina echoing through the hallways.

Marry me, Andrea. It's the only solution.

Promise me, Andrea. Promise you'll never leave Mayela.

Andrea massaged her temples with her fingertips, willing the voices away. "I'm tired," she said. "If you'll excuse me—"

She hurried out of the room, feeling their gazes digging into her back as she retreated. But at the bottom of the stairs, she hesitated. She had no idea where she was going.

Robert appeared behind her. "Take a right at the top of the stairs. Your room is the third door on the left."

Andrea turned to him gratefully. "Thank you."

"No problem. Come on. I'll walk up with you. I'm sure Dorian and Paul have a lot to talk about."

Andrea wondered what Richard's former mother-in-law and his current business partner might have to talk about, but if the possessive way Dorian had clung to the man's arm was any indication, their relationship was hardly business.

Paul Bellamy, however, had had eyes only for Andrea. She shivered as she climbed the stairs beside Robert.

"I imagine you're wondering about Dorian," he said.

"What do you mean?"

He trained his gaze on her. "She doesn't like you, you know."

"I gathered as much, but I have no idea why."

"For starters, you're young and beautiful," Robert said. "That alone is reason enough for Dorian to despise you, but then you had to go and commit the ultimate sin. You married Richard."

They paused at the top of the stairs, and Andrea glanced up at him. "You mean because I married him so soon after Christina's death?"

"No. I mean because Dorian planned to become the second Mrs. Malone herself." Robert turned and headed down the hallway.

Andrea, after absorbing this, rushed to catch up. "She wanted to marry her daughter's husband?"

He shrugged. "Dorian considered him fair game. Especially since she'd seen him first."

"I don't understand."

"Richard was in a relationship with Dorian when he met Christina. He fell in love with her instantly. Think how that must have made Dorian feel—her young, beautiful daughter stealing away her fiancé."

"They were *engaged*?"

"Oh, yes. Dorian was very bitter, as you can imagine. She's always carried a torch for Richard. When Christina died, I'm sure she thought she might have a second chance with him. Then you came along, another young, beautiful woman—and her granddaughter's nanny, to boot."

"I'm sorry," Andrea said, not quite knowing how to respond to all that he'd told her.

Robert grinned suddenly. "Don't apologize to me. You and I have always gotten along famously. You didn't kick *me* out when you and Richard got married."

"How long have you lived here?" Andrea asked.

"Off and on for years. Richard's been a good brother to me," he said, but his eyes didn't quite tell the same tale.

Andrea wondered if, in spite of his words, he resented Richard. Richard was the older, wealthier, more successful brother. It would only be natural if Robert felt twinges of jealousy from time to time.

"How long has Dorian lived here?" Andrea asked.

"She came after Christina died, ostensibly to help take care of Mayela, but she never left. She tried several times to move in before, but it never worked. She and Christina couldn't get along for more than a few weeks at a time."

"I see."

"Well," Robert said. "Here we are. This is your room." He waved toward the closed door in front of them. "Yours and Richard's."

Andrea stared at that closed door. Beyond would be evidence of her marriage to Richard. Proof that she was, indeed, married. A visual reminder that she wasn't free to love another man.

She thought of Troy and wanted to cry.

Instead, she put her hand out to open the door. "Thanks for showing me to my room."

"Will we see you at dinner?"

"I don't know. I may go to bed early," she said.

"Then I'll see you tomorrow. Good night."

"Good night."

She turned and opened the door.

Chapter Eleven

"I made a few calls after Dr. Bennett left this morning," Madison said.

Troy glanced at his sister. He'd gone back to her town house after dropping Andrea at the Malone mansion instead of going home to his empty apartment. He didn't want to spend the evening brooding about Andrea, and yet, no matter where he went or what he did, he couldn't stop thinking about her.

"What kind of calls?" He poured himself a cup of coffee, then turned to lean against the counter.

"Let me back up." Madison tucked her dark hair behind her ears. "After Dr. Bennett left this morning, I went searching through the attic for her book."

"The one you read in college?"

She nodded. "I knew there was something about it that fascinated me back then, but I couldn't remember exactly what." She picked up a hardcover book lying on the counter and handed it to Troy. "Notice anything unusual?"

Troy glanced at the cover—*Dark Journey,* by Dr. Claudia M. Bennett. He thumbed through the pages, skimming passages here and there. "Sounds like the usual psychobabble stuff to me."

"I'm not talking about the text," Madison said. "There's no picture of the author on the jacket."

"So?"

"It's intriguing to me because of what happened to Dr. Bennett. She used herself as one of her case studies in the book."

"Are you saying she was her own patient?" Troy asked skeptically. No wonder the woman had struck him as odd.

"In a manner of speaking," Madison said. "She'd only been out of med school a few years when she was attacked one night leaving her office. Two men dragged her into an alley where they beat and raped her. They left her for dead. After that, she became severely agoraphobic. At the time she wrote this book, she hadn't left her home in over ten years."

Troy glanced up. "She didn't seem to have that problem this morning."

"I know," Madison agreed. "That's why I put in a call to a few of my colleagues. I wanted to find out what I could about her before she began seeing Andrea again."

"Did you find out anything?"

"According to the grapevine, she's lived in Houston for less than a year. She moved here to teach a graduate course in behavioral modification at the university, though she still sees a few patients from an office in her home. Before that, she lived in New York, where she had a small practice, but spent most of her time writing and doing research."

"Any idea why she moved down here?"

Madison shrugged. "All I could find out was that she told the department chair at the university she needed a change. I have no idea how she found Andrea. Or how Andrea found her."

"I think I might know," Troy said. "Dr. Bennett also treated Christina Malone."

"The first wife?"

Troy nodded. "I looked over the file earlier. According to interviews conducted at the time of her death, Christina suffered from severe depression and had been seeing Dr. Bennett. She overdosed on prescription amphetamines."

"Were they prescribed by Dr. Bennett?"

"There was no evidence to that effect, and Dr. Bennett denied giving her any kind of medication."

"It's not that hard to get amphetamines," Madison said. "She could have gotten them anywhere."

"Yeah, but what I'd really like to know is why Andrea started seeing Dr. Bennett after that. Christina's suicide was hardly a glowing recommendation."

"You can't blame her suicide on her therapist," Madison said, automatically coming to the defense of a colleague. "You don't know all the facts, and besides, Dr. Bennett's credentials are impeccable."

"If they're so impeccable, why did you feel the need to check up on her?"

Madison shrugged. "Just to satisfy my curiosity."

"That's all?"

She hesitated. Her dark eyes clouded, but she shook her head. "She checks out, Troy."

"Maybe on paper. But if what you say is true, she lived through a pretty severe trauma herself. She was agoraphobic for at least ten years, yet this morning she didn't appear to have any difficulty being out and about. Could she recover from a phobia that easily?"

"We don't know that her recovery was all that easy," Madison argued. "Or how long it may have taken."

"Still," Troy said. "It's enough out of the ordinary to make me think we should keep digging."

Madison smiled wryly. "That's what I thought you'd say, and that's why I've already got a call into a friend of mine in New York. We should know more about Dr. Bennett in a day or two."

Troy was impressed by his sister's tenacity. "You'd have made one hell of a cop, you know that?"

There was a trace of regret in Madison's voice when she said, "I guess it's in my blood."

ANDREA WALKED AROUND the bedroom at least a dozen times, but there was nothing that seemed familiar to her—not the damask curtains at the windows, not the ivory-colored walls or the jewel green carpet. Not the lamps, not the chairs, not the heavy wood furniture. Not even the king-size bed with the bold paisley spread.

Especially not the bed.

When she'd first entered the room, her gaze had gone immediately to that bed, then she'd quickly glanced away, afraid to look. Afraid to awaken her sleeping memories. Afraid to think about her and Richard in that bed—

But she needn't have worried. When she finally got up enough courage to not only stare at the bed, but to sit on the edge, not a single memory was stirred. Not one. The bed was a sterile place for her.

How could that be? she wondered. She and Richard had been married for a month. Surely they must have spent the night together. Slept together. How could she not have memories of making love with her husband?

As Andrea explored the room further, she thought she'd found her answer. At least, it was the most plausible explanation she could come up with. The dressing room wedged between the huge master bathroom and the walk-in closet contained a cot. Andrea knew instinctively this was her bed. This was where she had slept.

But why?

What kind of relationship did she and Richard have? Why did they sleep in separate beds?

As Andrea lay down on the cot, her eyes fluttered closed and she found herself wishing that this was all some horrible mistake. She wasn't really married after all. Richard Malone wasn't her husband. She didn't have a husband. She was free to love another man.

She was free to go to Troy and tell him how she felt.

A powerful image swept over her then. Not a dream or a memory this time, but a fantasy. She and Troy, together in this tiny bed, arms and legs entwined, bodies pressed close. She could almost feel his lips at her throat, his hand skimming her thigh, his voice whispering in her ear exactly what he wanted to do to her. And her own heated reply, *Yes. Oh, yes.*

She snuggled deeper into the bed, not wanting to let go of the fantasy, but knowing all the while that it could never be anything more.

A LITTLE WHILE LATER, Andrea stood on the balcony off Richard's bedroom, watching dark clouds gather in the distance. She shivered in the waiting calm. The storm was hours away, but the thought of thunder and lightning crashing all around made her uneasy. Was she afraid of storms? She didn't think so, yet she couldn't shake her disquiet. Bad weather meant trouble.

Feeling unsettled by the approaching storm and by her ominous thoughts, Andrea decided to join the others for dinner after all. Mayela's little face lit when she saw her, and Andrea was glad she'd decided to come down.

But the child's joy was short-lived. By the time they went in to dinner, Mayela's shoulders were drooping and her eyes looked suspiciously bright.

"Don't slump, Mayela," Dorian scolded.

Mayela made a halfhearted attempt to straighten, then let her shoulders fall forward again.

"What's the matter?" Robert asked. "Too much soccer today?"

Mayela shook her head. "When's Daddy coming home?"

"You know very well he's not coming home until next week," Dorian said. "He's away on business."

"Why did he have to go away?" Mayela whined. "Why does he always have to go away?" She turned and gazed up at Andrea. Her eyes looked far too troubled for a seven-year-old. "He *is* coming home this time, isn't he?"

Andrea's heart quickened. It was almost as if the child knew something. "If he's away on business," she said carefully, "why wouldn't he come home?"

"You know why," Mayela said very softly. So softly that Andrea was certain Robert and Dorian hadn't heard her. Mayela turned back to her plate and sighed, as if the conversation had taken far too much of her flagging energy. "I'm tired. May I be excused?"

"You haven't eaten your dinner," Dorian said.

"I'm not hungry."

"Very well."

The child got up and stood beside Andrea's chair. "Will you come tuck me in?"

"Of course."

"Will you tell me a story?"

"If I can think of one." Andrea excused herself and pushed back her chair.

Upstairs, she sat on the edge of the canopied bed while Mayela brushed her teeth and got into her pajamas. Then she came and crawled into bed, and Andrea tucked her in.

"Tell me one of the keyhole stories," Mayela begged.

"I'm afraid I don't remember them," Andrea said. "Why don't you tell me one?"

"There was this little girl," Mayela began solemnly. "She was locked away in this dark room by her evil stepmother or somebody, and the only way she could see the outside world was through the keyhole in her door."

Andrea began to feel uneasy. She wished Mayela would stop, but the child warmed to the story. "The keyhole was magic, see. Every time the little girl would look through it, she'd see something different. One time she saw a beautiful garden with roses and lilies and bright yellow butterflies. Another time she saw great big crystal snowflakes that sparkled like diamonds in the sunlight."

"Sounds like a pretty neat keyhole," Andrea murmured. She was drowning. A cold darkness closed in on her.

"Tell me what the little girl sees now, Andrea. Make up something really neat. Please."

Blood, Andrea thought. *She sees blood.*

In her mind, she could see the little girl kneeling at the keyhole. But she couldn't see what the little girl could see. Andrea wouldn't let herself see beyond that door. She couldn't. Not yet. She wasn't ready.

Mayela waited impatiently. She tugged on Andrea's hand. "What does she see?"

"She doesn't see anything," Andrea forced herself to say lightly. "Do you know why?"

Mayela shook her head.

"Because she's sleeping. Just like you should be."

"But I'm not tired." Mayela smothered a yawn.

"You said you were downstairs," Andrea argued.

"Yes, but I just said that so you'd come up here with me. I don't like the way Dorian tucks me in, and she doesn't know any good stories."

"Why do you call her Dorian?"

Mayela shrugged. "She told me to. She doesn't like to be called Grandmother or anything like that."

"Is that why you called her Grandmother earlier?"

An impish smile tugged at the corners of the child's mouth. Andrea couldn't help smiling, too. She knew Mayela was probably a handful at times, but Andrea also knew that she loved the little girl dearly. She didn't have to remember that. She felt it every time she looked at Mayela's sweet little face. Andrea skimmed the back of her fingers along the child's downy cheek.

Mayela turned serious again, her blue eyes gazing up at Andrea in earnest. "You won't go away again, will you? Promise me you won't."

"I won't. Not if I can help it."

"Daddy said you'd always be here to take care of me. Even when he's not." Mayela hesitated. Her eyes clouded, and for a moment, she struggled with her emotions. "I'll be brave," she whispered, blinking furiously. "I promised Daddy."

"Brave about what?"

But Mayela said nothing else. She turned her head away, so Andrea couldn't see her tears. Andrea's throat constricted. She felt like crying herself. Mayela seemed to know something was wrong, just as Andrea knew. But *how* did they know? Why were she and Mayela the only ones who knew that Richard wasn't ever coming back?

Andrea gathered the little girl in her arms, and for a long moment, they rocked each other back and forth. Neither of them cried. Neither of them said anything.

But they both knew.

Mayela's daddy wasn't coming back.

Just as Andrea's daddy hadn't come back all those years ago.

ANDREA LAY IN THE DARK, her eyes wide, her heart hammering, as she listened for the noise that had awakened her. It came again, and for a moment, she thought someone was on the roof, trying to find a way to break in. Then she realized the storm had hit, and the sound she heard was tree limbs scraping against the shingles.

She got up and moved to the French doors that opened onto the balcony. The rain hadn't started yet, but the wind was up, whipping the giant trees that surrounded the house into a frenzy. Jagged lightning bolts split the sky in two places, and thunder rattled the windows.

Andrea stood outside, letting the wind tear through her hair. She wasn't frightened by the storm, but as earlier, an uncanny sense of unease plagued her. Something about the weather bothered her.

The rain came suddenly, in great sheets, and Andrea hurried inside and bolted the French doors. She stood watching the water drip down the glass as a torrent of memories buffeted her.

It had been raining that Sunday night. She remembered that now, and something urgent had driven her out into the weather. She closed her eyes, remembering the sound of the rain on her car roof, the almost frantic beat of the wiper blades against her windshield. She'd been running to someone, hadn't she? Or had she been running away?

Andrea strained to remember. Why had she been out driving that Sunday night? And why had the police picked her up walking? What had happened to her in the time in between?

She turned away from the window, distressed by all

the questions rumbling around inside her. As she moved toward her bed, a piercing scream stopped her in her tracks.

Andrea's heart leapt to her throat. It was as though the scream had come from inside her, a manifestation of her troubled thoughts and her unnamed fears. But as she stood listening to the sounds of the storm, the scream came again and again.

Mayela!

The child was afraid of the storm. That was why Andrea had been so uneasy all evening. She knew the approaching storm would frighten Mayela.

Andrea flew across the room and threw open her door. Mayela's room was in the east section of the house, across the bridge that connected the two wings. There was no light in the hallway, but Andrea didn't take time to look for a switch.

As she rushed across the bridge at the top of the stairs, she felt something wet beneath her bare feet. Her feet slipped from under her. She fell heavily against the stair railing and clung to the banister to keep from falling.

As she righted herself, she could feel water dripping down on her. The skylight directly over her had been broken by a tree limb, and rain cascaded downward, creating a treacherous puddle on the marble.

As Andrea continued to look up, she heard a terrible cracking sound. Then, almost in slow motion, the window gave way, and large sections of glass arrowed toward the floor. Toward her.

She had no time to think, to even breathe. Automatically she stepped back. Into nothing but air. For a moment, for an eternity, Andrea hung suspended at the top of the stairs. She was still looking up, and just before she tumbled backward, she could have sworn she saw a face in the gaping hole left by the falling glass.

Chapter Twelve

The drive to the hospital from Troy's apartment normally took twenty-five minutes. He was aiming for closer to fifteen. He made almost all the lights, and the ones he didn't make, he ran. An off-duty cop driving like a bat out of hell was a dangerous thing, and Troy told himself to slow down before he hurt some innocent bystander. His foot eased on the accelerator, but his heart pounded like a piston inside him. It had ever since Tim Seavers had called him from the emergency room to tell him that Andrea had been brought in a few minutes ago.

He hit the ER doors on the run, and the nurse at the desk told him where Andrea had been taken. He tried not to think about that first night, when he'd seen her in the hospital with blood all over her clothes. He tried not to remember the premonition he'd had then that a woman like her meant nothing but trouble for a man like him.

"Tim!"

Tim Seavers was coming out of one of the cubicles, and when he heard Troy call to him, he reversed course and came toward him. They stood in the hallway, oblivious to the noise and confusion around them.

"How bad is it?" Troy asked.

"Not as bad as it could have been." Tim jotted a few

notes on the chart he was holding, then looked up. "She has a few cuts and bruises, and she'll be sore in the morning, but other than that, she's one lucky woman."

Troy breathed a sigh of relief. "What happened?"

"I don't know all the details, but evidently she took a tumble down the stairs at her home. She managed to break the fall by grabbing hold of the banister. The EMTs said the place is a mess over there. Broken glass and water everywhere. You might want to talk to him." He nodded toward the waiting room where Robert Malone paced nervously.

"I want to see Andrea first."

"Would it do any good if I said no?"

"Not one damn bit."

Tim sighed. "That's what I figured. Go on, then, but just for a few minutes. I don't want her upset."

Troy had no intention of upsetting Andrea. He told himself as he stood looking at her through the curtains surrounding the cubicle that he would be gentle with her. He wouldn't question her too harshly. But what he heard come out of his mouth when she opened her eyes and looked at him was a gruff "What the hell happened?"

"Troy." There was a small bandage on her forehead, and another on the back of her hand. A faint bruise colored her right cheek, and her hair had been pushed back to reveal a deeper bruise at her temple.

Troy felt a curious sensation in the back of his throat that made it difficult to talk.

Andrea's eyes were shadowed as she looked up at him. "Is Mayela all right?"

He cleared his throat. "Why wouldn't she be? You're the one who fell down the stairs."

"I know, but—"

"But what?" He took her hand and held it in both of

his. He could feel her trembling, and he wanted to gather her in his arms, hold her close, tell her everything was going to be all right. But how could he tell her that when he didn't know what the hell had happened?

"Why are you so worried about Mayela?" he persisted.

"Because it could have been her here instead of me," Andrea said softly. "She could have been the one to fall, and if it *had* been her—" She broke off on a wave of emotion, as if she couldn't bear to think of the little girl's being hurt in any way.

"Just tell me what happened."

At first, Troy thought she would refuse. She withdrew her hand from his and turned her head to stare at the ceiling. Finally she said, "I heard Mayela scream. I knew she was afraid of storms so—"

"Wait a minute. How did you know she was afraid of storms?"

"I...remembered."

Troy gazed down at her. What else had she remembered? What else had she not told him? "Go on."

"I ran to her. Her room is on the opposite side of the house from...Richard's. The skylight at the top of the stairs had been broken in the storm. There was water all over the floor. I slipped, and then I saw all that glass falling toward me. I stepped back without thinking and lost my balance. But I could have sworn I saw—"

"What?"

She bit her lip. "It all happened so fast. I was so scared."

She was holding back again. Refusing to tell him the whole story. Frustrated, Troy ran his hand through his damp hair. "Why can't you trust me?"

Her blue eyes shone like stardust. "You don't know how much I want to."

"Then do it, damn it. Let me help you."

"I can't."

"Why not?" he demanded.

"Because it's not just me I have to protect," Andrea said desperately. "It's Mayela. I'm all she has left."

Something clenched in Troy's stomach. He stared down at her. Hard. "What about her father? She has him, doesn't she?"

A look of fear flashed in her eyes before she quickly turned away, so he couldn't see her expression.

"What did you mean by that, Andrea? Have you remembered something else?"

She shook her head. "It's...something Mayela said. I don't think her father is home very much. I don't think he spends much time with her."

"I see." More than she thought he did, Troy thought. She'd avoided using Richard's name. She hadn't called him her husband. Instead, she'd referred to him as Mayela's father. If that wasn't significant to Andrea, it sure as hell was to Troy.

Hope springs eternal, he told himself in disgust.

"You still here?" Tim strode into the cubicle and gave Troy a stern look. "My patient needs her rest, Sergeant."

"When can I go home?" Andrea asked anxiously.

"Tomorrow morning. I'm keeping you overnight for observation."

"But I'm fine," she protested. "I don't need to stay here overnight. I have to get home to Mayela."

"Who's Mayela?" Tim asked.

"My stepdaughter," Andrea said. "She needs me. I have to get home to her."

"You have to do what the doctor says," Troy said.

"But if it'll make you feel better, I'll go by the house and make sure she's all right." He'd been planning to go over there anyway and take a look at the situation for himself.

Andrea's eyes were still shadowed with worry. She grabbed Troy's hand and clung to it. "Tell them—tell them you're watching out for her."

"Tell who?"

"Dorian and Robert. Make sure they know you're watching them."

"Robert's in the waiting room now," Troy said. "Did he drive you here?"

"No. He called the ambulance, and then I guess he followed in his car. Dorian stayed home with Mayela."

"Do you want to see him?"

"No!"

Her vehemence startled Troy. He gazed down at her. "All right. I'll go out and have a few words with him before I leave."

Andrea clung to his hand for a moment. "Tell him what I said. Tell them both."

But by the time Troy walked out to the waiting room, Robert had already gone.

What was going on here? Why was Andrea so afraid—not just for herself, but for Mayela?

He told himself on the drive to the Malone house that a broken skylight in a windstorm was not an unusual occurrence and not something anyone could have planned on. But when he walked into the house, saw the location of the window and the amount of broken glass on the marble floor, he had to agree with Tim Seavers. Andrea was indeed one lucky woman. He wondered if she had any idea how close she'd come to being killed tonight.

The window had cracked just enough at first to allow

water to puddle on the marble floor. It was a wonder Andrea hadn't fallen the first time she'd slipped. If she'd injured herself then, she might not have looked up. And even if she had, she might not have been able to move out of the way in time to see the heavy glass window falling from the sky toward her. She might easily have been killed.

An accident? Maybe.

Maybe not.

Suddenly Andrea's concern for Mayela took on a whole new and ominous meaning. If a child had come running down that hallway, she would have undoubtedly slipped and fallen. She would have undoubtedly been lying there when the large sections of glass had broken loose.

Troy knelt and picked up a piece of the glass. The jagged point would have made a deadly weapon, and he hated to think what would have happened if Mayela had come along first. Or if Andrea hadn't moved out of the way in time.

He looked down from the bridge to find Dorian and Robert watching him. They were both in robes. Robert held a drink in his hand, and Dorian had lit a cigarette. They looked nervous, Troy thought, as if they had something to hide.

"I'd like to see Mayela," he told them.

"What on earth for?" Dorian asked coldly. "The child's asleep."

"She may have witnessed the accident." Troy stood and brushed off his hands, his gaze lingering on the broken glass. Then he glanced down at Robert and Dorian, and his expression hardened. "I want to find out tonight, from her, exactly what she saw."

* * *

WHEN TROY ARRIVED at the hospital the next morning, Andrea was already up, dressed and ready to go.

"How are you feeling?" he asked.

"Not bad. A little sore." She tentatively moved her left arm, which had taken the brunt of her fall. She was lucky she hadn't broken it. Lucky she hadn't broken her neck. "Did you see Mayela last night?"

"Yes. She seemed fine."

"Thanks." Andrea looked around, suddenly uneasy at the effect Troy's presence was having on her. She felt more vulnerable this morning than she had in a very long time. He crossed the room to stand in front of her, and Andrea's breath caught in her throat as she gazed up at him.

"I'm going to ask you a question, and I want you to tell me the truth." His eyes were dark and deep and more than a little suspicious.

Andrea swallowed. "What is it?"

"You don't think what happened last night was an accident, do you?"

She shifted her gaze, unable to meet his eyes.

"Don't do that," he said.

"Don't do what?"

"Look away from me. Try to hide your feelings from me. We've come too far for that, Andrea."

They had come too far. Further than they'd had any right. That was the problem.

She sighed. "I don't know if last night was an accident or not. I don't have any proof that it wasn't. No real proof," she added softly.

"What's that supposed to mean?"

"Just that..." She turned to the window and stared out. "Last night, before I fell, I was still looking up at the skylight. I could have sworn..."

"What?"

"I...thought I saw someone looking down at me."

She waited for sounds of his disbelief, braced herself for his skepticism, but his explosion stunned her. "Why didn't you tell me this last night?"

"Because I didn't think you'd believe me," Andrea said. She turned to face him. "Think about it, Troy. I'm not exactly the most credible witness right now."

He started to argue with her, but stopped himself because there was merit in what she'd said, and they both knew it.

"You still should have told me," he said. "How can I help you if you don't level with me?"

"I'm sorry. But it all happened so fast, I couldn't be sure of what I saw. I'm still not sure."

"Well, one thing's for damn sure," Troy said grimly. He paced the room, deep in thought. "You can't go back to that house. Not until we find out what the hell is going on."

Andrea watched his every movement. "I have to go back," she said. "I can't leave Mayela there alone. She needs me."

Troy glanced up, his expression dark. "Then get her out of that house, too. Bring her with you."

"How? You're a cop, Troy. You know there isn't a judge in the world who would allow me to remove that child from her home in my present situation. I don't have a choice. I have to stay there until..." Andrea trailed off, not wanting to mention her husband's name, not wanting him to come between them once again.

But Troy had no such compunction. "Until what? Until Richard comes home?" He stopped his pacing and stared at her. "What happens when your husband does come home, Andrea?"

"What do you mean?"

His gaze deepened. "I mean what happens to us."

"Troy—"

"Tell me something." An angry glint appeared in his eyes. "How do you feel when you hear his name? What did you remember when you slept in his bed last night?"

Andrea knew that if she was smart, she would tell him it was none of his business. She would do nothing to add fuel to the fire that had ignited between them, but instead she said very softly, "I didn't sleep in his bed last night. I slept in my own bed."

Dead silence fell over the room.

Andrea released a long breath. "I don't sleep with my husband. We have separate beds."

Troy's gaze was almost too intent to bear. "I find that very hard to believe."

"It's true," Andrea whispered. "I don't love him, Troy."

"How can you know that? If you don't remember him, how can you know that you don't love him?"

"I don't remember Mayela, either, but I know that I love her dearly."

An emotion that might have been hope flickered in Troy's dark eyes, but he quickly dashed it away by saying, "I think what you're experiencing is an amnesia that's even more selective than we first thought. Is it possible you've told yourself you don't love him, made yourself believe it because of...us?"

"I *don't* love him," Andrea insisted. "And I didn't marry him for his money."

"I never said you did."

"But you've thought it. You know you have, and I don't blame you. I know how all this must look to you, but...I think I married Richard because of Mayela."

"Mayela?"

Andrea nodded. "She said something last night that started me thinking. Richard isn't home much. He travels all the time, and maybe after Christina died, he needed someone to take care of Mayela."

"You were already taking care of her. You were her nanny."

"I know, but maybe Richard thought she needed a mother."

Troy still wasn't convinced. "That doesn't explain why *you* would agree to something so drastic, unless—"

She cut him off. "Unless I was getting something in return? But I *was* getting something. Don't you see? I was getting Mayela. Maybe I needed her as much as she needed me. I don't seem to have any other family."

"It's possible, I guess." He ran his fingers through his hair. "Hell, anything's possible."

"Then you believe me?"

"I believe it's what you think," he said carefully.

Not good enough. She wanted him convinced. She wanted him to believe wholeheartedly, as she did, that she had never been in love with Richard Malone, and that she wasn't the type of woman who would have married him for his money. She wanted Troy to believe the best about her. It was the most important thing in the world to her at that moment. "I wasn't in love with Richard," she said almost desperately. "Because if I had been, I couldn't feel the way I do about you."

Troy didn't say anything to that, but he took her hand and pulled her into his arms. They stood that way for a very long time, and Andrea wasn't sure if the embrace would have eventually led to more. If she would have had the willpower to stop him from kissing her.

She never had the chance to find out. She became

aware of such a strong malevolent presence in the room with them, that at first she thought it might actually be Richard's ghost. Then she looked up to see Paul Bellamy glaring at her from the doorway.

Troy saw him at the same time and released her, but he kept one arm around her waist.

Paul walked into the room, his handsome features like chiseled granite. "What's going on in here?"

Andrea's glance fell to the flowers he carried in one hand. White roses. Her favorite. "What are you doing here?" she asked, not liking the way Paul Bellamy was looking at her. Not liking the memory of his kiss.

"I heard about what happened last night from Dorian. I wanted to make sure you were all right. I can see that you are," he said, tossing the roses onto her bed.

Andrea eased away from Troy's arm and felt him stiffen beside her.

Andrea said weakly, "This is Paul Bellamy. He's Richard's partner."

"I'm Sergeant Stoner," Troy said. "HPD." The two men didn't shake hands.

"So you're here in an official capacity?" Paul asked, but his eyes told them he already knew the answer.

Troy ignored the insinuation and the question. "I've been trying to get in touch with you, Mr. Bellamy, but you haven't returned any of my phone calls."

"I thought you were trying to get in touch with Richard," Paul said, casting a meaningful glance at Andrea, as if to remind them just who Richard was.

"Your secretary said there's no way to get in touch with him."

"That's right. There isn't."

"He doesn't check in with the office?"

"No. That's the whole point of his little trip. There's

no way any member of the group can contact civilization. They're completely isolated.''

"So actually you have no way of knowing whether Richard is with the group or not," Troy said. "Is that right?"

Paul Bellamy hesitated, as if caught off guard by the question. "Why wouldn't he be with them? The whole thing was his idea."

"Are you in charge of the company while he's gone?"

"I'm the president and CFO," Paul said. "But I really can't see where all these questions are leading, Sergeant. Andrea had an unfortunate accident last night, but as I understand it, that's all it was. Is there any reason why I can't take her home this morning?"

"Maybe you should ask *her* that question," Troy said.

Andrea felt both sets of male eyes on her, and she was about to inform them that she could find her own way home. But just then, Troy's cellular phone rang, and he fished it out of his jacket pocket to flip it open. He turned his back to Andrea, but she heard him say his name into the phone. Then he listened for a moment and finished with a curt "I'll be right there."

He disconnected the phone and dropped it in his pocket as he turned back to Andrea. "I have to go." There was a look of urgency in his eyes, and Andrea couldn't help wondering what the call had been in reference to. Was it something to do with her?

A chill crept up her spine, and she shivered.

"You okay?" Troy asked, still gazing down at her.

Andrea nodded. "I'm fine."

He seemed reluctant to leave. He looked as if he wanted to say something else, do something more, and for a moment, Andrea held her breath. Would he kiss her in front of Paul Bellamy?

A trace of regret flashed in Troy's eyes. "I'll be in touch," he said. Then he brushed past Paul Bellamy and disappeared out the door.

AS IT TURNED OUT, Andrea was forced to accept a ride home with Paul after all. There seemed little point in calling a taxi when he was standing in the same room making the offer. Still, there was something about him that made Andrea extremely uncomfortable. She hated how he kept looking at her and the possessive way he took her arm to help her into his car.

Once they were on the road, Andrea stole a glance in his direction. He was very handsome, with finely molded features and a well-honed body that most women would admire, but there was nothing in the least appealing about him to Andrea. Instead, she found his excessive good looks a little unsettling, as if they disguised the real man beneath.

As if reading her thoughts, he flashed her a smile that should have ignited her pulse, but didn't. Andrea turned to look out the window.

"You don't have to keep pretending," he said. "Not with me."

Reluctantly Andrea turned to face him. "I don't know what you mean."

"This memory thing. I don't know what you're trying to pull, but you don't have to keep up the game with me."

Andrea glared at him. "It's not a game. I don't remember you. I don't remember anything about you."

His features hardened, and suddenly he didn't look handsome at all. "You expect me to believe that? After what we had?"

Her stomach tightened in fear. "We...had a relationship?"

Paul shot her a look. "You couldn't have forgotten. There's no way."

Andrea didn't think she wanted to hear any more, but she couldn't seem to stop herself from asking, "Was it...before....?"

One brow rose. "Before you married Richard? It started before."

She looked at him in disgust. "You mean—"

"You really don't remember, do you? I guess it wasn't as good for you as it was for me." He laughed, a low, rumbling sound that set Andrea's stomach to churning.

She couldn't stand to hear any more. She didn't want to find out anything else about herself, about Paul Bellamy and about what had happened between them.

She'd convinced herself that what she felt for Troy was a once-in-a-lifetime thing. A pure and wonderful thing. The reason she could be married and have feelings for him was that what they felt for each other was so very special. Love at first sight.

But now the thought of her and Paul Bellamy...

Andrea's skin crawled. Whether she'd loved Richard or not, she couldn't stand the thought of having betrayed him, especially with a man she knew she *couldn't* have been in love with.

She felt as if she'd betrayed Troy, too.

At that moment, Andrea hoped she never got her memory back. She hoped she never had to find out the kind of woman she'd been. Because what if she became her again?

Tears stung behind her lids, and she squeezed her eyes closed. But even as she tried to keep the memories at bay, one struggled frantically to get out. The image formed against Andrea's will, and she was powerless to stop it.

She could see the anger in Paul's eyes as he grabbed her arm and hauled her up against him. He kissed her roughly, and Andrea pulled away. She tried to slap him, but he caught her wrist and held it so tightly she cried out.

"I never thought you'd go through with it. I never thought you'd actually marry him. But now that you have, it's only fair I get what I want."

"I don't know what you're talking about," Andrea said, her heart tripping with fear inside her. *Paul Bellamy was a monster. He'd do anything to get what he wanted.*

"I want what's rightfully mine. You owe me, damn it. You're nothing but a tease," he said in contempt. *"All these months you've been leading me on...."*

"I never led you on," Andrea whispered aloud.

He glanced at her and smiled as he pulled into the Malone driveway. "So you remember that little conversation we had at the reception, do you?"

Andrea felt chilled as she watched him. He stopped the car, cut the engine and turned to her, draping one arm over the steering wheel.

"What else do you remember, Andrea?"

"Nothing." She edged toward the door, felt the handle against her side. "I just know I never led you on. We didn't have a relationship. Why did you try to make me think we did?"

"Oh, we had a relationship, all right. And I'll bet you remember a hell of a lot more about it than you're letting on. Maybe all you need is something to jog your memory."

Before Andrea had time to react, he reached for her,

pulled her roughly against him and kissed her, just as he had once before. Andrea shuddered, but not in pleasure. Not with desire. She was frightened and disgusted and she wanted to claw his eyes out. She raked her fingernails down the side of his face, and Paul shoved her away.

"Damn you." He put a hand to the angry red marks on his cheek. He looked furious enough to hit her, and Andrea jerked open the door and tumbled out. She fled up the steps to the front door, pushed it open and ran inside.

Dorian was just coming down the stairs. She paused, her gaze moving over Andrea's shoulder. Her dark eyes narrowed as Paul Bellamy appeared in the doorway. "What are you doing here?" she asked.

"I drove Andrea home from the hospital." Except for the scratches on his face, he might have stepped straight from the pages of *GQ*.

The scratches did not go unnoticed by Dorian. She took in Paul's rigid demeanor, Andrea's disheveled appearance, and a look of cold rage hardened her features.

"Where's Mayela?" Andrea said stiffly. "I'd like to see her."

"She's already left for school," Dorian said. "I drove her there myself."

The thought of Mayela alone in a car with Dorian Andropoulos was unsettling. Andrea said, "Then if you'll excuse me, I'd like to go up to my room."

As Andrea passed her on the stairs, Dorian caught her arm. "Enjoy it while you can," she said softly. "I have a feeling things are about to change around here."

Andrea shrugged loose from the woman's grip without reply. She had more to worry about than Dorian's cryptic remarks.

At the top of the stairs, Andrea paused, gazing up at

the skylight. The window had already been repaired, the glass swept up, the floor cleaned and, she suspected, the tree limb cut up and carted away. Someone had been very efficient this morning. If a crime had been committed, the evidence had all been cleared away. There was nothing left to remind Andrea that she had almost been killed last night.

Nothing except the memory of that face staring down at her from the broken skylight.

Chapter Thirteen

Richard Malone had been shot three times in the chest, point-blank. Overkill, Troy thought, gazing down at the body. The first bullet to the chest had undoubtedly taken him out. The second shot had been insurance. The third, rage. Or revenge.

By the time Troy arrived at the airport parking lot following Lucas's call, the trunk of Richard Malone's Mercedes had been popped and his body, which had been found encased in a plastic bag, had been removed and was lying on the pavement. The CSU team was all over the car, and the medical examiner was busy with the body. A few feet away, a rookie noisily lost his breakfast. Richard Malone had been dead for several days. He wasn't a pretty sight.

"Parking stub on the dash is dated a week ago last Sunday, 8:26 p.m.," Lucas said. "Looks like someone plugged him, bagged him and then drove him here to the airport, where they knew it might take a few days for his car to be found. How does that square with the time Andrea Malone was found that same night?"

"She was brought to the hospital just before midnight," Troy said.

"Plenty of time," Lucas said. "Even if she had to get

a cab back from the airport, she'd still have had time to get dropped off, maybe even change back into the blood-stained dress and then wander around for a few minutes until someone picked her up and took her to the hospital. If she had an accomplice, it would have been even easier.''

An accomplice? An image of the way Paul Bellamy had been looking at Andrea earlier this morning rose in Troy's mind. "You're assuming she's been faking her amnesia," he said. "You're assuming this was all a carefully calculated plan on Andrea's part."

"Someone sure as hell calculated it," Lucas said grimly. "You know as well as I do that the spouse is always the number-one suspect."

Troy stared down at Richard Malone's body. Was it possible Andrea had killed him? Was she capable?

Or, as Lucas had suggested, did she have an accomplice? Someone willing to do anything for her—even commit murder?

Troy didn't want to believe it, and yet he couldn't help remembering the way he'd been taken in by Cassandra Markham.

"I'm sending a team over to the house this morning," Lucas said. "We've got to move fast on this thing. We've already lost over a week. Whatever evidence might have been recovered has probably disappeared by now."

"Give me a chance to break it to the family first," Troy said. "Malone had a kid."

Lucas nodded. "Go ahead. It'll take us a couple of hours to get the warrant."

TROY WISHED he had been able to be alone with Andrea before he broke the news to the rest of the family, but there wasn't a chance. Dorian and Robert were in the living room when he arrived, and the maid was sent to fetch Andrea. Troy was glad that Mayela was still at school.

Andrea looked a little pale when she appeared in the doorway, and when Troy suggested she take a seat, her face became even more drawn. Dorian and Robert were seated on the sofa, and Andrea chose a chair away from them. She seemed to have a hard time meeting Troy's gaze, as if she somehow knew why he was there.

"There's no easy way to say this," he began. "Richard's body was discovered in the trunk of his car this morning at the airport. He'd been shot. The coroner thinks he's been dead since a week ago Sunday night."

Out of the corner of his eye, Troy witnessed Dorian's and Robert's reactions. Robert grew very still. His eyes closed against the terrible news, while Dorian gasped in shock. She covered her face with her hands and sobbed.

But it was Andrea who captured Troy's attention. She, too, grew very still, but her blue eyes were wide open and they contained not even a shadow of surprise. When she saw that Troy was staring at her, she cast her gaze downward. But it was too late. He'd already seen too much.

Andrea had known, before Troy ever arrived, that Richard Malone was dead.

IT WAS DECIDED that while the forensics team went over every square inch of the Malone house, Connie Perelli, the mother of Mayela's best friend, would pick both girls up at school and take them to her house so that Mayela wouldn't have to witness the police search.

Andrea, looking even paler than she had earlier, told Robert and Dorian that she wanted to be the one to tell Mayela about Richard, and though Troy saw the contempt glittering in Dorian's dark eyes, she reluctantly agreed. Meanwhile, Robert, looking visibly shaken, accompanied an officer to the morgue to positively identify the body.

By the time Troy and Andrea left the house, Forensics had gathered several dozen packets of evidence, but nothing that looked very promising. Still, Troy thought, you never knew what the lab might be able to come up with.

At the Perelli home, Andrea went upstairs to talk to Mayela alone, and Troy was left downstairs with Mrs. Perelli.

"Call me Connie," she said nervously as she sat on the edge of the sofa, wringing her hands. "That poor child. I can't imagine what this will do to her. First her mother, and now Richard—" She broke off, biting her lip as tears sprang to her eyes.

"How well did you know Richard Malone?" Troy asked.

Connie Perelli dabbed at her eyes. "Not well. He traveled a lot. He was hardly ever home. I'm afraid he was little more than a stranger to Mayela. He never came to any of her school functions. Andrea was always the one who attended the parties and sat through the plays. Even before Christina died, Andrea and Mayela were inseparable."

"You knew Christina Malone?"

"We were good friends at one time. I can't tell you how shocked I was when she committed suicide."

"I understand she'd been suffering from depression for quite a while before her death."

Connie's eyes filled again. "That's true. But she wasn't always like that. I remember a time when Christina was truly happy, full of life. She was deeply in love with Richard, even though he was so much older than her. I think it really hurt her that he was always so wrapped up in his business. She hated the way he ignored Mayela. She told me once she thought the only reason he agreed to have a child with her in the first place was so she would have something to keep her occupied while he was gone."

"Is that the reason she became depressed?" Troy probed gently.

"Not altogether. At least I don't think so. I think part of it had to do with her mother."

"Dorian Andropoulos?"

Connie nodded. "They never got along. Christina used to get so depressed after one of Dorian's visits. She'd mope around in a blue funk for days. Then the depression started lasting longer and longer, until, toward the end, Christina hardly ever left her room, except to see Dr. Bennett."

"You knew about Dr. Bennett?"

"Christina wasn't ashamed of seeing a therapist. She wanted to get help. She wanted to get better."

"Do you happen to know how she met Dr. Bennett?"

"I don't remember if she ever said."

Troy paused. "You say you and Christina Malone were once close. How did you feel about her husband remarrying so soon after her death?"

Connie gave him a stern look. "You've been listening to Dorian, haven't you?"

"I beg your pardon?"

Connie's thin lips tightened in disapproval. "Look, I know she doesn't like Andrea. Dorian's accused her of some pretty rotten things, like marrying Richard for his money and all that, but...I don't think it was that way."

Troy tried to keep his tone professional when he said,

"You think Andrea was in love with Richard Malone? Is that why she married him?"

Connie hesitated. "I don't know Andrea very well. She keeps to herself, and she's certainly never confided in me. I don't know whether she was in love with Richard or not, but I can tell you this. She loves Mayela as if she were her own child. There's a bond between them that, in some ways, is even stronger than the one between a natural mother and daughter. I don't know what would have happened to that poor little thing after Christina died if it hadn't been for Andrea. I don't know what would happen to her now—" Connie broke off on another wave of emotion, and Troy gave her a moment to compose herself.

"Before today, when was the last time you saw Andrea?"

She didn't have to give it much thought. "A week ago Sunday night. Mayela spent the night with Lauren, and Andrea drove over to bring Mayela a little teddy bear she always sleeps with. She said she knew Mayela would have a hard time falling asleep without it, but the real reason she came was because of the bad weather. Mayela's scared of storms, I mean really terrified, and Andrea wanted to make sure she was all right."

"How long did she stay here that night?"

"Not long. She left before seven. She said she had to see someone."

"Did she say who it was?"

"No. But if it hadn't been something pretty important, I know she would never have left Mayela."

The picture Connie Perelli painted of Andrea was very different from the way Dorian Andropoulos had portrayed her. Troy wondered if he could trust either view.

* * *

"How did she take it?"

"It was so strange," Andrea said. They were sitting alone in the Perelli living room. "She didn't cry, she didn't even act that surprised. She just sat there looking so sad."

Not unlike Andrea's own reaction, Troy thought. He studied her as she sat with her head against the back of the sofa, her eyes closed, her fingertips massaging her temples. She looked indescribably weary, and the tiny lines around her eyes and mouth were more pronounced than he had ever seen them.

He stared at her and thought, *I don't know you. I may be falling in love with you, but I don't really know you.*

He wondered if he ever would.

Troy left Andrea at the Perelli home, then drove over to Dr. Bennett's house a few blocks from River Oaks. A housekeeper answered the door and ushered Troy inside. She glanced at his badge and ID. "Do you have an appointment?"

"No. But I have some information I think Dr. Bennett would be interested in hearing. Is she in?"

"I'll tell her you're here."

A few minutes later, the housekeeper returned and showed Troy to Dr. Bennett's office. "She'll be down in a moment. In the meantime, make yourself comfortable. Please excuse the paint fumes," she said. "We're in the middle of redecorating."

"So I see." Troy glanced around at the sheet-draped furniture.

"We had a little accident a few nights ago," she told him. "A water pipe broke in the wall. Dr. Bennett's office was completely flooded. I've never seen such a mess."

"Sergeant Stoner?" Dr. Bennett walked into the room, looking very much the way Troy remembered her. She was dressed in a conservative brown suit, a cream-colored blouse and low-heeled shoes. Her dark hair was pulled back from her face, and her complexion was covered with heavy makeup. She took a seat behind her desk and dismissed the housekeeper with a curt nod.

"You're here about Richard, no doubt."

Troy looked at her in surprise. "You've heard?"

"It's all over the news, Sergeant. Apparently someone from your office leaked the story to the press right after the body was found."

Figures. "I guess you're wondering why I'm here."

She smiled slightly. "Not really. Both of Richard's wives were patients of mine. One of them still is. I'm not surprised you'd want to talk to me, although I must remind you of the confidentiality agreement between doctor and patient."

"Christina Malone is dead," Troy said. "You're no longer bound by that agreement."

"Maybe not legally, but I still have a moral obligation to protect my patient."

"And I have an obligation to find out who killed Richard Malone," Troy said grimly. "I need to know why Christina Malone was seeing you."

One dark brow rose. "I don't see how knowing that would help you."

"She committed suicide six months ago, and now her husband has been murdered. There may not be a connection between those two deaths, but then again, there just might be. And if there is a link, you could be the one person who can help me find it. Now, if I have to get a court order to get into your files, I'll do it. But wouldn't it be easier if you just told me what I need to know?"

Dr. Bennett paused to consider what he'd said. Then she nodded briefly. "All right. Christina Malone came to me because she was experiencing severe depression. Her marriage was in deep trouble."

"Why?"

Again Dr. Bennett paused. "She believed her husband was having an affair. With Andrea Evans."

Troy felt as if someone had punched him in the gut. The wind left his lungs with a painful swoosh, and it was a struggle to keep his voice from giving away his shock. "That didn't create a conflict of interest for you?"

"Not at all. Andrea didn't come to me for help until after Christina was dead."

"Did she…tell you anything that bore out Christina's fears?"

"I'm afraid I can't discuss Andrea with you, Sergeant. She's still my patient."

"How did you meet Christina Malone? Did someone refer her to you?"

"Actually we met quite by accident. We shared an affinity for primitive art, and we met at a gallery last summer. We got to talking, and she asked if she could come to see me professionally."

"Is that the usual way your patients find you?"

Annoyance flickered in her blue eyes. "I don't solicit, if that's what you're inferring. I knew something was troubling Christina. I wanted to help her."

"Did you prescribe amphetamines for her depression?"

"I did not. The police asked me that question at the time of her suicide. I don't believe in drug therapy, Sergeant."

"You didn't prescribe sleeping pills for Andrea?"

"Of course not. Why would you ask?"

"The night she was brought in to the hospital, the lab found trace amounts of a drug used in sleeping pills in her blood."

Dr. Bennett shook her head. "I'm not surprised. Andrea has a great deal of trouble sleeping. She suffers from nightmares."

"Is that why she came to see you?"

A look of alarm flared in her eyes, as if she'd said more than she intended. Then she said carefully, "The nightmares brought her to me, but she had...other concerns she wanted to talk about, things that were triggered by Christina's death."

"Such as?"

Dr. Bennett swiveled in her chair and stared out the window for a long moment, as if debating with her own conscience. Finally she sighed and turned back to Troy. "When Andrea first came to see me, she couldn't recall much about her past before the age of ten. It was as if her childhood was a complete blank, with occasional flashes of memory that were as troubling to her as they were confusing."

"What do you mean?"

"Andrea was convinced she'd done something wrong as a child. That's why she was sent to live with an aunt who didn't love her. That was her punishment."

"For what?"

"We were just getting to that."

"How?"

"By using regressive hypnosis. Little by little, we were putting together the pieces of Andrea's past, and then this happened. Her current amnesia is a severe setback."

"When's the last time you spoke with her?"

"A few days ago. At your sister's house."

"I mean before that."

"A week or two."

"You didn't see her a week ago last Sunday night?" She looked surprised. "No."

"She was going to see someone after seven o'clock in the evening. It was a matter of importance."

"It wasn't me, Sergeant. I rarely keep weekend hours, only in cases of extreme emergency. Andrea and I always met on weekday afternoons. She wanted to be finished with our sessions before school let out, so she could pick up Mayela."

"Your sessions concerned only her past?"

Silence.

"She didn't discuss her marriage?" Troy persisted. "She didn't talk about her husband?"

Dr. Bennett leaned back in her chair and eyed him coolly. "I've already said much more than I should have, Sergeant."

"I understand. And I appreciate your cooperation. Just tell me one more thing," Troy said. "Do you really believe Andrea has amnesia?"

Dr. Bennett considered the question for a long, tense moment. Troy felt as if he were sitting on the edge of his seat, waiting for her answer. He forced himself to relax and observe Dr. Bennett as dispassionately as she studied him.

She smiled, as if reading his thoughts. Or more likely, his body language. "You've been with her more than I have in the past few days, Sergeant Stoner. What do you think?"

Just like a shrink to turn his own question back around to him. Troy got up and walked over to the window. "My sister showed me the book you two were talking about the other day."

"Did she?"

Troy turned to face her. "She told me about your condition. The agoraphobia. At the time you wrote *Dark Journey,* you'd been confined to your house for more than ten years. Is that right?"

She gave him a wry look. "I don't see what that has to do with your case."

"It doesn't. I'm just curious. How did you get over something like that?"

"Are you familiar with the term 'flooding,' Sergeant Stoner?"

"You aren't talking about what happened to your office, I take it."

"In psychiatric terms, flooding is an extreme method of dealing with fear. A patient is forced to confront the thing he's afraid of most." She toyed with a pencil on her desk. "When I was confined to my home, my worst fear was that I would someday be forced to face my attackers again, that if I were to leave the protection of my home, they would be lying in wait for me and they would kill me. If not them, then someone else. The outside world became a very dark and dangerous place for me, a world in which I simply could not cope."

"How did you continue your profession?" Troy asked.

"My office was in my home, much like this," she said. "I saw very few patients back then, and only referrals. I wrote books and papers, and concentrated almost solely on my research into behavioral modification. I had a housekeeper, a wonderful woman, who did everything for me. She was my companion, my friend and my buffer against the outside world. I don't know what I would have done without her, because at the time, I was quite certain I would never again leave my home."

"What happened?"

"One night a fire erupted in the house. The flames were everywhere, the smoke so thick I could hardly breathe. Even then, with my life hanging by a thread, and the firefighters trying to battle their way inside to save me, I didn't think I could make myself crawl toward their voices. My fear was that great. But in the end, my instinct for survival won out, and I was forced to confront my fear."

"The housekeeper you talked about," Troy said. "Was she the same woman I met earlier?"

Dr. Bennett glanced away. A look of genuine distress crossed her features. "No. Marlena wasn't as lucky as me. She died in the fire. In fact, the police said the blaze started in her room. She fell asleep while smoking a cigarette. Ironic, isn't it, that she should be the one to be trapped inside that house instead of me?"

Chapter Fourteen

The autopsy was performed on Richard Malone immediately. Troy met with the coroner, Dr. Nguyen, the next morning to determine the exact cause of death—a technicality in this case, considering the extent of damage wrought by the bullets.

Dr. Nguyen launched into the medical specifics with gusto before Troy held up his hand to stop him. "Just tell me if you found anything unusual in the autopsy. Anything I should be aware of."

"We did find something interesting," Dr. Nguyen said. "Richard Malone's death resulted from the gunshot wounds he sustained to the heart, no question. But if the killer had waited, the victim would have been dead in six months anyway."

Troy glanced up. "Meaning?"

"Richard Malone was dying of liver cancer."

"Did you know Richard was dying?"

Dorian stared at Troy in shock. *"What?"*

"Richard was dying of liver cancer. The coroner said he would probably have been dead within six months. Did either of you know?"

Dorian visibly paled. She sat down heavily on the sofa, her eyes dark with disbelief. "That isn't possible."

"It's true," Troy said. He turned to Robert Malone, who had poured himself a stiff drink at the bar.

Robert's hand trembled as he lifted the glass to his lips. "Richard never said a word to me." His voice was raspy with shock. "I had no idea. Perhaps he didn't know."

"He knew," Troy said. "His personal physician corroborated the coroner's report, as did his lawyer."

"Lawyer?" Dorian's gaze suddenly became more alert, as did Robert's. The two of them reminded Troy of vultures, picking at the remains.

"He met with his lawyer shortly after he and Andrea married. According to his attorney, Richard was getting everything in order in preparation for his death. He made Andrea his daughter's legal guardian, and he cleared the way for her to eventually adopt Mayela."

If possible, Dorian grew even paler, but her dark eyes flashed with rage. She jumped to her feet, her long red nails curled into claws. "That's ridiculous. I'm the child's grandmother."

"And I'm her uncle," Robert said. "But I agree with Richard. Mayela belongs with Andrea."

"Over my dead body," said Dorian. "That woman isn't fit to raise a child, certainly not my granddaughter. She may have schemed her way into this house and into Richard's affections, but she doesn't fool me. I know how to deal with her kind."

"Watch yourself," Robert advised.

Dorian ignored him. She pointed a finger at Troy. "Andrea Evans murdered Richard. You know it as well as I do. Why haven't you arrested her?"

"This is an ongoing investigation," Troy said. "We're still gathering evidence. We have more than one suspect, Mrs. Andropoulos."

"You're protecting her," Dorian accused. "I've seen the way you look at her. You've fallen for her just like every other man who comes into contact with her. You all make me sick."

"Dorian," Robert warned.

She turned on him. "Don't 'Dorian' me. You're no better than the rest of them. I've seen you lust after her, too. Your own brother's wife. But she didn't give you the time of day, did she? And do you know why? Because you're not Richard. You're nothing but a washed-up drunk who'd gamble away his own mother's last cent if you got the chance."

Robert didn't say anything to that. He lifted his glass and took a long drink, but Troy could see that his hands were still shaking badly, and his skin tone had deepened to a dull red. Dorian had humiliated and angered him, but Troy suspected she'd also hit a little too close to the truth.

A movement out of the corner of his eye caught Troy's attention, and he turned. Andrea stood in the foyer, just beyond the doorway. She made no move to join them, but he could tell from her expression that she'd heard everything they'd said, including Dorian's accusations.

Without a word, she turned and walked back up the stairs.

ANDREA STOOD on the balcony off Richard's room and watched Troy drive away. She hadn't spoken to him downstairs because she hadn't known what to say. How to defend herself against Dorian's accusations. How to respond to the knowledge that Richard had been dying of cancer before he was murdered.

A chill of unease crept over her. Had she known? She must have, because Troy said that Richard had made her Mayela's legal guardian, that he'd taken steps for her to adopt the little girl. Andrea had to have known, but who else had Richard told?

Suddenly she remembered something Mayela had said the first night Andrea had been back. *Daddy said you'd always be here to take care of me. Even when he's not.*

Mayela had known, too. That must have been part of Richard's preparations. He hadn't wanted her to experience the same kind of shock she'd gone through when her mother had died so suddenly. He'd wanted to make it as easy for his daughter as possible, even going so far as to finding her a mother.

Andrea's heart tripped inside her. If she had known that Richard was dying, didn't that let her off the hook as a suspect? Why would she kill him if he was dying? If she knew she would eventually get what she wanted?

If you didn't kill him, how did you know he was dead before the police found him? a little voice in the back of her mind asked. *Why were you covered in blood that night?*

THE FUNERAL on Saturday morning was a terrible ordeal. Andrea sat listening to Richard's eulogy, holding tightly to Mayela's little hand and wondering what the child must be feeling. She seemed so resolved on the outside, so stoic. But the world-weary expression in the little girl's eyes broke Andrea's heart. She was all Mayela had left, and Andrea's own resolve strengthened. She would do whatever she had to do to protect her.

But for how long? Dorian was the child's grandmother. Would she have more rights than Andrea? Even though Richard had made her the legal guardian, would a court uphold his wishes? Or would Dorian, the child's next of kin, be awarded custody?

Two days later, on Monday morning, Andrea sat in the lawyer's office with the same fears and waited for the reading of the will. Across the room, Dorian, dressed in widow's black, stared at Andrea through the mesh veil of her hat. The woman's hostility was almost a tangible thing, and Andrea shivered, realizing again how very much Dorian hated her.

Robert sat next to Dorian, but the two were hardly allied. They hadn't spoken since Robert had come into the room a few minutes ago and taken his seat. He stared straight ahead, his hands gripping the arms of his chair. Today he wasn't even pretending to be relaxed. He was as tense as Dorian, and not once had he bothered to glance in Andrea's direction.

Paul Bellamy arrived late and sat behind Andrea. He made no move to touch her or to even speak to her, but Andrea could feel his eyes on her. The skin at the back of her neck crawled, and it was all she could do not to get up and leave. She didn't belong here. What was she doing with these people?

Finally the lawyer walked into the room, took his seat behind his desk and, with a flourish, took out Richard's will. His gaze swept the room, making them all wait breathlessly. Then his eyes lit on Andrea, and he said, "Mrs. Malone, Richard has appointed you as executrix of his estate and as such, you will have full control of all assets, including the partnership in Malone International, until the child reaches the age of twenty-one."

Andrea sat stunned. She'd hoped and prayed that Mayela would be left in her care, but to be put in charge of Mayela's fortune? What did Andrea know about managing an estate that large? What did she know about anything? A few short days ago, she hadn't even known her own name.

The lawyer must have sensed her distress. "Rest assured, Mrs. Malone, that this law firm will help you in any way we can. Perhaps you'd like to come back in a day or two when things have settled a bit and we can talk further."

Andrea nodded, but she still felt numb as she listened to the rest of the will. Richard's legacy was quite simple. Mayela inherited almost everything—the cash, the real-estate holdings, the stocks and bonds and Richard's partnership in Malone International.

Dorian got nothing.

Robert got nothing.

Paul Bellamy got nothing.

"And to my wife, Andrea Evans Malone, I bequeath the sum of ten million dollars."

Andrea gasped, the only sound made in the otherwise tomblike office. Ten million! Surely there must be some mistake. She and Richard had only been married a few weeks. Why would he leave her an amount so large? Why would he leave her anything, for that matter? They hadn't really been husband and wife, had they? They'd slept in separate beds.

Why had he made her his daughter's legal guardian and the executrix of his estate? Why had he had so much faith in her?

And why had he been killed?

A dark premonition descended over Andrea. Richard's

bequest made her look even more guilty. No one else had benefited from his death. No one except Andrea.

Dorian jumped to her feet. Fury contorted her face into an ugly mask. Her nostrils flared, her lips curled and Andrea thought the woman looked almost bestial in the cruel overhead lighting.

"You won't get away with this," she said. "I'll fight you for Mayela. There isn't a court in this country that would allow my granddaughter to be raised by a murderess. I'll make sure of that."

She grabbed up her purse and stalked out of the room. Paul Bellamy followed close behind, and Andrea wondered what strategy the two of them might be cooking up.

The lawyer rose, too, and picked up his briefcase. "If you'll excuse me, I'm due in another meeting. Call me in a day or two," he said to Andrea.

For an awkward moment, Andrea and Robert were left alone in the office. She wondered what he was thinking. There was an odd glint in his eyes that disturbed her. Then he shrugged, and the carefree Robert surfaced once again. "Congratulations."

An odd thing to say, Andrea thought, in light of his brother's death.

Robert shook his head. "I never thought he'd cut me out like that. He always threatened to, but I never thought he'd do it. When push came to shove, he was always there to bail me out. I thought surely—" He broke off, shaking his head again.

"What will you do now?" Andrea asked.

Robert shrugged again. "Get a job, I guess. Find an apartment. I'll get by. I always do. Don't worry about me."

"What about Dorian?" Andrea asked.

"What about her?"

"Will she stay in Houston?"

"Oh, she'll stay, all right. She won't give up Mayela without a fight. Don't make the mistake of underestimating her, Andrea. Dorian can be ruthless. I've seen her in action," he said bitterly. "She won't let anything stand in her way. Not you. Not even Mayela."

Andrea felt chilled all of a sudden. "Are you saying she's dangerous?"

"I'm saying she'll do whatever it takes to get what she wants. I wouldn't like to be in your shoes right now," he said cryptically before he turned and walked out of the room.

Andrea stood in the empty office, feeling so completely alone. The weight of her responsibility pressed down on her. She was thankful that Mayela would remain with her, at least for now, but the money...all that money was an invitation to trouble.

Maybe even to murder, she thought with a shiver.

She was suddenly glad that Mayela had gone to spend the night with Lauren Perelli and her family. It would give Andrea a chance to make other living arrangements for them, because one thing was certain. She didn't want Mayela going home to that mansion. Not while Dorian and Robert were still there.

In spite of his warning about Dorian, Andrea didn't trust Robert, either. She'd seen the greed and desperation in his eyes today when he learned he'd been cut from Richard's will. How far would *he* be willing to go to get his hands on his brother's money?

A few minutes later, Andrea stepped outside the building into the blinding glare of the sun. She put up a hand to shade her eyes just as someone grabbed her arm and spun her around. Andrea gasped when she saw Paul Bellamy's dark expression. No wonder he'd left the lawyer's office behind Dorian. He'd been lying in wait outside.

"We have to talk." He clutched her arms, his expression more urgent than angry.

"What about?"

"You know damn well what about. The partnership should be mine. I've worked my ass off for that company. If it wasn't for me, Malone International would have gone down the toilet years ago while Richard blithely conducted his little survival missions and executive-training courses. I'm the one who made that company what it is today. Malone International is mine, and neither you nor anyone else is going to take it away from me."

The desperate look in his eyes frightened Andrea. She was glad they were standing on a public street, in plain view of passersby.

"I don't know anything about running a company," she said, trying to appease him for the moment. "There's no reason why things have to change at Malone International. You'll still be in charge."

"I'm glad you're being so reasonable." His expression altered subtly. His gaze deepened and dropped to her lips. "I like it when you cooperate."

Andrea shuddered, hating his touch. Hating the fact that she may have once invited that touch. She lifted both hands to shove him away when she glimpsed a familiar face on the street.

Troy!

Troy looking at her in disgust. Troy seeing her in Paul Bellamy's arms and thinking the worst.

Troy turning and walking away.

* * *

TROY HADN'T BEEN ABLE to get the image of Andrea and Paul Bellamy out of his head all day. He stood on the balcony of his apartment and sipped his drink as he watched twilight deepen to darkness. He couldn't help remembering the possessive way Bellamy had acted toward Andrea that day in her hospital room, when he said he'd come to take her home. Troy had sensed something was going on then, but he'd told himself it was probably nothing more than his imagination. His own possessive feelings toward Andrea kicking in.

After today, he wasn't so sure. They'd been standing so close, she and Bellamy. Right out there on the street. And Bellamy had been touching her.

Troy's grip tightened on his glass. He'd hated seeing Andrea like that. He couldn't stand the thought of her being with another man. Not Paul Bellamy. Not Richard Malone. Not anyone but him.

You're a fool, Troy told himself as he refilled his glass from the whiskey bottle he'd carried outside. But that admonishment didn't stop him from wondering what Andrea was doing at that very moment.

Was she alone, like him? Or was she with Paul Bellamy? Were the two of them celebrating tonight? Richard was dead, and Andrea now controlled his millions. For all Troy knew, this had been her game plan all along. Hers and Bellamy's. If they'd been having an affair, that gave them both the perfect motive for murder.

But even as Troy devised the scenario in his head, there was one thing he couldn't quite resolve. The way Andrea felt about Mayela. The way she was so protective toward the little girl.

Could that be an act, too?

Maybe, but he was hard-pressed to believe anyone

could be that good an actress. It had been his experience that kids weren't easily taken in. If Andrea was putting on an act, if she wasn't genuinely fond of Mayela, the kid would know it. But Mayela seemed to return her affection wholeheartedly. She obviously loved Andrea as much as…

He did.

Damn. Falling in love with a suspect was never a good idea.

He finished off the last of the whiskey in his glass and poured himself another drink. The doorbell rang, and Troy considered ignoring it. He didn't feel much like company tonight, but then he figured, what the hell? If he stayed out here all night, he'd just get drunk, and then he'd have to drag himself out of bed in the morning and feel like crap for the rest of the day. Wasn't worth it.

But when he drew back the door and saw who stood on the other side, he thought again how a woman like her was nothing but trouble for a man like him.

Andrea saw the drink in his hand and looked at him uncertainly. "Am I…interrupting something?"

"No. Come on in." He stood back while she entered, then closed the door behind her. "Would you like a drink?"

"No, thanks. I don't drink."

"A little something else you remembered?" He knew his tone sounded accusing, but damn it, he couldn't help it. Who did she think she was, coming over here like this, looking all soft and feminine and vulnerable? He wondered if she had an idea the picture she made standing in his living room, wearing a black knit dress and pearls and dark stockings that made him want to—

He shook his head, as if to clear away the sudden image of Andrea in black satin. Andrea in his bed.

The image wouldn't fade. Troy wondered if he'd had more to drink than he realized. If his control had been weakened by the whiskey.

Or by the woman.

Lifting his glass, he took another drink, studying her over the rim. He couldn't figure out how she'd found his apartment, but at the moment, the effort to ask her was just too great. He was tired of asking Andrea questions. Tired of never getting the answers he needed. With Andrea, he felt as if he were always walking a tightrope in fog. He couldn't see where he was going, and one false step could be his downfall.

"I guess you know about the will," she said finally, when the silence had stretched on for too long.

"I'm conducting a murder investigation. It's my business to know."

She nodded. Her gaze dropped to the drink in his hand, and for a moment, she seemed fascinated by the swirling amber liquid inside. Then she said softly, "I didn't kill Richard."

"I never said you did."

"But you must be thinking it. All that money—" She broke off and walked to the open balcony doors to stare into the darkness. "I didn't kill him. I couldn't have. I'm not that kind of person...am I?" She turned to face him then, and her eyes looked haunted, desperate. Troy thought he saw a glimmer of fear in those crystalline depths. Or was that wishful thinking on his part? He'd never been able to tell with Andrea.

He set his drink aside and slowly crossed the room

toward her. But he didn't dare touch her. "Why did you come here tonight?"

She wrapped her arms around herself. "I don't know. I needed to see you."

"Why?"

"You're the only person I can talk to." She took a deep, shaky breath. "There're so many things I don't know about myself. I don't know who I really am, or what I might have done in my past. I have these horrible nightmares. I see blood all over my hands. Oh, God—" She broke off and closed her eyes, as if overcome with emotion. A tear trickled down her cheek, and it was all Troy could do not to reach for her and wipe it away.

She opened her eyes and gazed up at him, her lashes starred with tears. "I know I don't have any right to ask you this, but...will you hold me? Just for a little while. I'm so scared, Troy."

The last was said on a whisper, and Troy felt something slipping away inside him, the last vestiges of his control. He wondered why he didn't feel more concerned. Why he wasn't trying to fight his feelings for her. Maybe it was too late for that anyway. Maybe it had been too late the moment he'd first laid eyes on her.

He took her hand and pulled her into his arms.

But if he'd meant to comfort her, that notion fled the moment he touched her. He tunneled his fingers into her hair and tilted her head back, so that for a split second, they were gazing deeply into one another's eyes.

And then he kissed her.

Andrea's lips trembled beneath his, then opened like a flower, inviting him to taste the sweetness inside. Troy groaned, wishing he'd never met this woman. Wishing he'd known her all his life. He was a cop, she was a suspect and they were both headed for trouble. But nothing could stop the heat between them. Not his job. Not her past. Not even the uncertainty of their future.

She pressed her body close to his, and passion exploded between them. Troy didn't think he could ever get enough of her. She was like no woman he'd ever known, and the desire roaring through him was like nothing he'd ever experienced. He wanted her. All of her. Now. And forever.

Her fingers were busy with the buttons on his shirt. Impatient, Troy ripped them loose, tossed the shirt aside, then reached for her once more. They kissed, again and again, breaking apart only when he found her zipper and lowered it. Her dress slipped to the floor. She was wearing stockings with black lace tops, and Troy's heart threatened to beat its way out of his chest.

A little voice in the back of his mind whispered to him this might be a planned seduction. Andrea might have come here to lure him more deeply into her web.

He ignored that voice.

He ignored his conscience and good sense.

He let her perfume, something dark and sultry, wrap around him like a silken scarf, drawing him more and more deeply into the fantasy. Slowly, their gazes clinging, he knelt and lowered her stockings from her sleek legs. She trembled when his fingers skimmed her thighs, touched her softly. Her head fell back, and she whispered his name on a sigh.

Troy stood, then lifted her into his arms and carried her into the bedroom. Moonlight silvered her hair as she lay atop the sheets, watching him undress. Then she held out her arms for him, and he moved over her, staring down at her for a long, breathless moment.

"Is this wrong?" she whispered, her eyes glowing with subtle mystery. Troy thought he could easily drown in those eyes. He could easily lose himself in her essence.

"It's the only thing in this whole damn mess that seems right," he muttered. And then he lowered his head and kissed her. Kissed her until nothing else mattered except the way she came to him so eagerly. The way she clung to him so desperately.

The way she shuddered in ecstasy when he took her.

ANDREA SIGHED. Curled on her side, her head resting on Troy's chest, she could hear the deep, even rhythm of his heart as it slowed back to normal. He had one arm around her, and his other arm was sprawled across the bed. His eyes were closed, and he looked replete. Satisfied. But not quite as relaxed as he might have been, Andrea thought. He still had doubts about her. Even after what they'd shared. Even after she'd given everything to him. He still had doubts.

What else could she do to convince him of her innocence?

Try the truth, the little voice in the back of her mind suggested.

She sighed again, and Troy stirred. His arm tightened around her. "What are you thinking?"

"I was just thinking that…I've never felt this way before. I don't know how I know that, but…" She turned to rest her chin lightly on his chest, gazing up at him. "I do know it."

Troy smiled, but his eyes were shadowed. "Why is it I want to believe you so badly?"

"You do?"

The shadow in his eyes deepened. "You do realize what I've done, don't you? What we've done?"

She lifted her head to stare down at him. "What do you mean?"

He sat up in bed, shifting ever so slightly away from her. Andrea felt chilled by his action.

"When you came here tonight…when I let you stay. I compromised the investigation, Andrea. My entire career could be on the line because of what we've done."

Andrea drew the sheet around her, bereft. "Are you sorry we made love?"

His eyes softened a little. He reached for her hand. "No. I'm not sorry. I've never felt this way, either. What happened between us was…incredible. But I have to know…I have to make sure you're being completely honest with me."

"I am." But she couldn't quite meet his eyes.

He took her chin, gently forcing her to look at him. "You told my mother that you remembered you were named after your grandmother, but you didn't tell me. You told my sister about the aunt who raised you, but you didn't tell me. I can't help wondering what else you might have remembered that you haven't told me."

After everything they'd shared tonight, the closeness they'd experienced, Andrea wanted more than anything to open up to him, to tell him about the dreams and the memories she'd been having. She wanted to tell him about Richard, how she had known, somehow, that he was dead before Troy had come to the house that day.

And she might have been able to tell him once, but not now. Not after the reading of Richard's will. Ten million dollars was a lot of money. A fortune. People had killed for a lot less. Andrea had to be the police's chief suspect. *Troy's* chief suspect.

If he found out she'd been withholding the truth from him, he'd have no reason to believe her about anything. It wouldn't matter that she knew in her heart she was innocent, because everything else, even her own memories, pointed to her guilt. And even though Troy might have compromised the investigation tonight, he was still a cop. He'd still have to do the right thing. If he thought her guilty of murder, he'd have to arrest her. Take her away, and there would be no one to protect Mayela.

"I've laid everything on the line for you, Andrea. All I'm asking is that you do the same," he said softly.

Andrea had never seen eyes so dark and deep. So very compelling. But God help her, she still couldn't tell him. Not even after tonight.

Not even knowing what it would cost her when he found out the truth.

Chapter Fifteen

The phone awakened Troy the next morning. He woke up groggy, his head filled with cobwebs, his memories of last evening hazy. He'd dreamed about Andrea, about the two of them in his bed—

The phone screamed again, peeling away the last layers of sleep. As he reached to answer it, Troy's memory sharpened and he realized it hadn't been a dream after all. Andrea really had been there. They'd made love.

But where was she now? He gazed at the empty side of the bed as he brought the receiver to his ear. "Hello?"

"Troy, it's Leanne."

"Leanne. Don't tell me you're already at the station." He propped himself on his elbows and squinted at the clock. It was only a little after five. Where the hell was Andrea?

"Don't tell me you're still lollygagging in bed while I'm down here working my butt off," Leanne snapped. "I've got some information for you."

"About the Malone case? What'd you find out?"

"I think you better get down here and see for yourself."

"I'll be there in twenty." Troy hung up and headed for the shower, but then detoured into the living room and kitchen, looking for Andrea. The path of clothing they'd left from the living room to the bedroom was gone. Even Troy's clothes had been picked up, and he found everything folded neatly on a chair.

Andrea had run out on him.

"WHAT'VE YOU GOT, LEANNE?"

She looked up and smiled smugly as Troy approached her desk. "I hardly know where to begin."

"That sounds promising." He pulled up a chair and sat down.

Leanne retrieved a folder from her desk and opened it, thumbing through the pages until she found the one she wanted. "Let's start with the mother-in-law. Dorian Andropoulos, formerly Dorian Kouriakis. She's Greek American, born in the Bronx, but she moved to Athens several years ago. Worked for the American embassy for a while, then married a shipping tycoon named Dimitri Andropoulos, an Onassis type, who even had a daughter named Christina."

"Wait a minute," Troy said. "You mean *he* had a daughter named Christina? Dorian wasn't her mother?"

"Stepmother. Christina was twelve years old when Dorian and Dimitri married. He died in some sort of freak boating accident two years later. The daughter inherited the fortune, but Dorian controlled the money until Christina turned twenty-one. Dorian moved back to the States almost immediately, and Christina was shipped off to boarding school in Switzerland until she was eighteen, at which time she met and married Richard Malone."

She handed the folder to Troy, and he glanced through the contents with interest.

"Another little tidbit you might find interesting," Leanne said. "While Christina was in boarding school,

Dorian managed to go through quite a bit of her step-daughter's inheritance. She'd already hooked herself a rich fiancé by the time Christina found out about the money. Only problem was, the rich fiancé married the daughter, and Dorian was left out in the cold.''

"Dorian was engaged to Richard Malone before he married Christina?''

"Bet that didn't sit too well with Dorian.'' Leanne grinned. She swiveled her chair and picked up another file. "Next on your list was Robert Malone. The brother.''

"I can hardly wait to hear this,'' Troy said, amazed at the amount of information Leanne had managed to dig up. It would have taken him weeks to assemble this much data.

"Likes to gamble,'' Leanne said. "Vegas, the Bahamas, and now the new casinos over in Mississippi and Louisiana. Rumor has it, he's in pretty heavy with some loan sharks.''

"Somehow that doesn't surprise me,'' Troy said, but it would explain why Robert might be feeling a little desperate, now that he'd been cut out of his brother's will.

Another thought occurred to Troy. If Dorian Andropoulos had been Christina Malone's stepmother, that meant Robert Malone was Mayela's next of kin. In a court battle for custody of the heiress, a blood relative might be given special consideration. Troy wondered if this possibility had occurred to Robert Malone, as well. Somehow he thought it probably had.

"Paul Bellamy,'' Leanne said. "Partner and CFO of Malone International. One of the employees over there leaked some information to a reporter friend of mine at the *Herald,* who was kind enough to pass the info along to me. It seems Richard started an in-house investigation a few months ago. He suspected someone close to the top at M.I. was embezzling pretty heavily from the coffers.''

''Paul Bellamy?''

''The employee didn't name names, but as chief financial officer, he'd certainly have control of the purse strings.''

And with Richard out of the way, Paul Bellamy would have a chance to cover his tracks before the feds moved in. Interesting. It appeared more than one person had a motive for wanting Richard Malone dead.

''That brings me to the last name on your list. Andrea Malone.'' Leanne opened the folder and glanced up. ''Boy, Stoner. You sure know how to pick 'em, don't you?''

''What do you mean?''

She pushed the file across the desk toward him. ''See for yourself.''

Troy opened the folder and stared down at a photocopied newspaper picture of a handcuffed woman flanked by two police officers. The caption read Evans Charged In Husband's Brutal Slaying.

The woman in the picture looked exactly like Andrea.

Troy's heart banged against his chest. Sweat trickled down his back, and for a moment, he thought he might actually be sick. Then he glanced at the date of the newspaper article. It was twenty years old. The woman in the photo looked to be in her late twenties, the same age as Andrea now. There was no way that woman could be her.

He glanced up, wondering if Leanne had noticed his strong reaction. If she did, she let it pass. ''That's Andrea's mother. Julia Evans.''

"What happened?"

"She went nuts one night and stabbed her husband twenty-seven times. According to the police report, Andrea was in the house at the time. They found her locked in a closet in some sort of trance. She wouldn't talk for days, and when she finally did, she acted as if she didn't remember anything about the murder. But the cops on the scene suspected she'd witnessed it. The closet was right off the room where her father was killed, and it had one of those old-fashioned locks, the ones with the big keys. They figured she could have seen the whole thing through the keyhole. Can you imagine what something like that would do to a seven-year-old kid?"

Troy could imagine, all right. When that kid grew up, she would have horrible nightmares and visions of blood. She would become adept at blocking memories that were too painful to recall.

As a man, Troy's heart went out to her. As a cop, he had to ask himself what else she might do.

"What happened to the mother?" he asked.

"She's been a resident at Oak Haven Hospital, twenty miles north of Houston, for the last twenty years. In case you hadn't figured it out," Leanne said, "Oak Haven is a mental institution for the criminally insane."

ANDREA HADN'T SEEN her mother since that awful night twenty years ago when Andrea's whole world had been shattered into a million pieces. Pieces that wouldn't be put back together for years and years to come.

But last night, after she and Troy had made love, after she'd given him her heart and her soul, she'd remembered. She'd fallen asleep in his arms and dreamed about the keyhole, the one Mayela had told her about. But in her dream, Andrea was the little girl who had been locked away in the dark room. She was the one kneeling at the door, looking through the keyhole, seeing all the blood. She was the one who heard her father's tortured pleas, her mother's demented laughter and her own terrified screams.

Andrea was the one who had looked through that keyhole and now she remembered.

Her mother had killed her father. Stabbed him so many times Andrea had lost count as she'd watched through the keyhole, screaming for her mother to stop, screaming for her father to get up, screaming because she'd been so bad that day, her mother had locked her in the closet and Andrea was powerless to help her father. He'd lain so still and lifeless, his clothes covered in blood.

"I hate you! I want you dead! Dead! Dead! Dead!" her mother had screamed.

Andrea had screamed, too. "You killed my daddy! You killed my daddy!"

Her father had been the only person in the world who had ever loved her. He never locked her in the dark room. He never told her she was bad.

When he died, Andrea had been all alone.

She closed her eyes briefly as the years of loneliness swept over her now. Tears stung behind her lids, and all she could think as she stood in the hallway at Oak Haven Hospital and gazed at her mother through the thick glass panel in the door was *Why? Why did you do it?*

Memories, long suppressed, rushed through Andrea. For twenty years, she had blocked the image of her mother's face. She wouldn't even let herself remember her father. All she knew was what her aunt had told her. Something terrible had happened to Andrea's parents. Her aunt hadn't wanted to be burdened with an orphaned niece, and so she had looked at Andrea accusingly whenever she'd spoken vaguely of the tragedy. Because of that, Andrea had assumed that whatever had happened to her parents was her fault. The feeling of guilt had been overwhelming at times.

A tear trickled down Andrea's cheek, and she hastily wiped it away with the back of her hand. She hadn't even known until recently that her mother was still alive. Andrea had assumed her dead all these years, even though her aunt had always referred to her as "away." Why else would her mother never have called or written? Now Andrea knew the truth.

"Would you like to go in and see her?" Dr. Albrecht, the physician who ran Oak Haven, asked softly.

Andrea hesitated. "I'm not sure."

"It's perfectly safe, you know. She won't harm you."

"It's not that...I'm not frightened for my safety."

"I understand." He gazed at her kindly through his wire-rimmed glasses. "It's been a long time, hasn't it?"

Andrea's throat tightened. "I didn't even remember her until recently. I didn't remember...what had happened." *What she'd done.*

"I've often wondered about her family." Dr. Albrecht stroked his chin thoughtfully. "In the twenty years she's been here, she's only had one visitor. Her sister came shortly after Julia was admitted."

"Aunt Clarice came here?"

"She explained to me that she had taken in her sister's child, and she wanted to make sure Julia's illness wasn't hereditary."

Andrea swallowed. "What did you tell her?"

The kindly eyes gazed down at her. "I told her it wasn't. Julia's illness is rare, one in a million. A brain malfunction that causes violent behavior during seizures.

Her condition is treatable but not curable. I'm afraid she'll never be able to leave Oak Haven.'' He paused for a moment, letting Andrea digest everything he'd told her. ''Would you like to go in now?''

Andrea nodded. Her heart pounded as Dr. Albrecht opened the door and she followed him inside. Her mother was sitting in a chair by the window, gazing out. She turned and her blue eyes—eyes so like Andrea's—lit with pleasure when she saw the doctor.

''I've been waiting and waiting,'' she said in a breathless voice.

''Sorry I'm late,'' Dr. Albrecht said cheerfully. ''But I've brought you a visitor. This is Andrea.''

Reluctantly Andrea stepped forward, and Julia clapped her hands excitedly. ''She's come to see *me?* Just *me?*''

''Just you,'' Dr. Albrecht said. ''I'm going to leave you two alone now, okay?''

Julia nodded eagerly and got up from her chair. She came toward Andrea, and Andrea had to resist the urge to retreat, to turn and follow Dr. Albrecht outside. Her heart beat so painfully against her chest, she felt dizzy.

''How long can you play?'' Julia asked anxiously.

''I...beg your pardon?''

''Would you like to have a tea party? Everything's ready. See?'' She pointed to a corner of the room where a small wooden table had been set with a toy tea service. ''Come on,'' she urged, reaching for Andrea's hand.

In spite of herself, Andrea drew back. She wasn't yet ready for physical contact with her mother. She wasn't sure she ever would be.

''What's the matter?'' Julia pouted. ''You don't like tea?''

"I—I love tea," Andrea stammered. "Why don't you pour me a cup?"

While Julia went off to pour the imaginary tea, Andrea gazed around the room. She'd been too nervous to notice before, but now she took in the stuffed animals on the single bed, the collection of dolls on the wooden dresser, the stack of board games in the corner. By all indications, Julia Evans had reverted back to her childhood.

She crossed the room and carefully handed Andrea the plastic cup and saucer, then waited impatiently until Andrea lifted the cup and tasted the "tea."

"It's very good," Andrea said, and Julia beamed. In spite of her illness and her confinement, the years had actually been kind to Andrea's mother. She was still quite lovely, with short, silky blond hair, wide blue eyes and a smooth, ivory complexion. She wore jeans and a bright blue T-shirt that made her seem young and innocent. To look at her, one would never guess what she had done. She was so happy and cheerful, so eager to please. She wasn't at all like the woman Andrea remembered.

This time, when Julia reached for her hand, Andrea let her take it and lead her across the room to the table.

OAK HAVEN HOSPITAL was located north of the city in a little bedroom community that had sprung up around a handful of high-tech firms opting out of the city. Troy had driven up right after he'd spoken with Leanne, and then with Lieutenant Lucas. After he'd met with the lieutenant, Troy knew it was imperative that he talk to Julia Evans's doctor. The similarities between the murder of Andrea's father and Richard Malone's death couldn't be ignored, no matter how much he might wish to.

Julia Evans had viciously murdered her husband in a

fit of uncontrollable rage. But at the time of her arrest, she claimed she could remember nothing of the attack. She went completely off the deep end and had to be confined to a private psychiatric hospital rather than be sent to prison or to the electric chair.

Twenty years later, Andrea's husband had been brutally murdered, and Andrea had been found with blood all over her clothing. Troy had learned this morning that the preliminary DNA testing proved conclusively the blood was Richard's. Yet like her mother, Andrea could remember nothing.

Or could she?

Troy had long suspected that Andrea remembered more than she'd told him. Question was, what was she hiding? And why?

As he pulled into the tree-shaded driveway of the hospital and showed his ID to the guard at the gatehouse, a chill of unease descended over him. Could Andrea be completely faking her amnesia? Had she followed her mother's example to keep from going to prison?

Was she capable of murder?

He thought about the woman he'd held in his arms last night. The woman who had enthralled him with her beauty. Her passion. Her mystery. He'd fallen in love with that woman, but he really didn't know her. He didn't know what she was capable of.

His unease continued to mount as he entered the hospital and spoke with a nurse at the front desk. He told her who he was, what he wanted, and she got on the phone to summon a Dr. Thomas Albrecht. A few moments later, Troy was ushered into Dr. Albrecht's office by a young woman who offered him coffee, which he declined.

Dr. Albrecht stood when Troy entered his office and reached across his desk to shake hands. "How may I help you, Sergeant Stoner?"

"I'm investigating a homicide which, in a roundabout way, involves one of your patients. Julia Evans."

Dr. Albrecht's brows lifted in surprise. "Julia Evans hasn't left these premises in twenty years, Sergeant."

"I realize that. It's her daughter, Andrea Evans Malone, I'm interested in."

"I see," was Dr. Albrecht's only comment, but something indefinable glimmered in his eyes.

"I've studied Julia Evans's file," Troy said. "According to the records, you were appointed by the court to give her a psychiatric evaluation. You testified at the trial that extensive testing had revealed an abnormality in Julia's brain which caused seizures, and that her violent behavior the night she murdered her husband was due to one of those seizures."

"That's correct," Dr. Albrecht said. "Her condition is rare. I've only heard of one other case similar to hers in all the years I've been a doctor." He steepled his fingers under his chin and regarded Troy thoughtfully. "The homicide you spoke of involving Julia's daughter. Can you tell me about it?"

"Her husband, Richard Malone, was murdered a week ago last Sunday night. Andrea was found wandering down a busy street that same night with blood all over her clothing. She didn't know who the blood belonged to or how it had gotten on her dress. She remembered nothing about her life, her past. She couldn't even remember her own name."

Dr. Albrecht's brows rose again. "Fascinating."

"At the time of her arrest, Julia Evans claimed she had amnesia," Troy said.

"Not amnesia," Dr. Albrecht clarified quickly. "Hers was not the normal repression of a traumatic event. Not even hypnosis or sodium Pentothal could help her remember, because the memories simply weren't there. Her brain had stored nothing of the savage attack on her husband."

"Which brings me to the reason why I'm here," Troy said. "Is there a chance Julia Evans's daughter could have inherited her...condition?"

"There is not."

"You sound pretty sure of that."

"I'm absolutely positive. Julia's illness is not hereditary. In fact, I suspect she sustained a severe brain trauma, perhaps as a child, that caused the abnormality, and hence the seizures."

Relief flooded through Troy, though he tried his damnedest not to show it. He was just a cop investigating a homicide. The fact that Andrea was the chief suspect couldn't be allowed to matter.

But, of course, it did. He was only human, after all.

"I think you can see why the similarities in the two cases would concern me," Troy said. "The violent nature of the murders and the loss of memory in both mother and daughter."

"You say Andrea claims to remember nothing of her life?" Dr. Albrecht picked up a pen from his desk and examined the tip, a casual movement, but something in his tone alerted Troy.

"That's what she claims, yes. Do you have reason to believe otherwise?"

Dr. Albrecht hesitated. He set the pen aside and

glanced up at Troy. "It might interest you to know, Sergeant Stoner, that I saw Andrea not more than fifteen minutes ago. She came here to see Julia."

The implication was not lost on Troy. If Andrea was suffering from amnesia, how did she know where to find her mother?

ANDREA LOOKED UP from Julia's tea party and saw Troy watching her through the glass panel in the door. Her heart bumped against her chest, then settled back into its normal rhythm. She supposed she shouldn't be surprised that he had found her here. He was a cop, after all.

She got up from the table, and Julia looked up at her in alarm. "You aren't leaving, are you? We're having so much fun."

"I know, but it's time for me to go home."

"Okay, but will you come back to see me?" her mother asked hopefully.

Andrea didn't quite know how to respond. She wasn't at all sure she'd be able to come back for another visit. She didn't know what would happen to her when her memory came back in full.

"I'll try," she promised.

Dr. Albrecht opened the door, and Andrea stepped out into the hallway. He went inside Julia's room, and Andrea and Troy stood silently for a moment. Then he took her arm and said, "Let's go outside where we can talk. Dr. Albrecht said there's a garden somewhere around here."

They found the garden near the rear of the hospital, enclosed in a wrought-iron fence shrouded with wisteria. They entered through the gate and sat down on a stone bench. The shaded garden was like a cool oasis, but the quiet was in direct contrast to the turmoil inside Andrea. Everything had happened so quickly. The memories had come so fast and furious, she'd hardly had time to think about what they all meant.

And now Troy was staring at her with dark, accusing eyes. Eyes that demanded an explanation.

Andrea couldn't look at him. "I guess you know about my mother. About what happened...back then."

"I saw the file this morning."

She closed her eyes as the memories washed over her again. "After...it happened, I was sent to live with my aunt. I couldn't remember anything about my mother and father except that something bad had happened to them. My aunt made it very clear that she didn't want me, and I assumed it was because whatever had happened was my fault. So I didn't try to remember. I found it much easier to forget." Her emotions were still so near the surface, she had to guard against tears. But she wouldn't let herself cry, no matter what. The last thing she wanted from Troy was his pity.

"Your aunt didn't talk to you about it?"

Andrea shook her head. "Aunt Clarice avoided the subject. If I asked her questions, she would always tell me I was better off not knowing, that I was lucky I couldn't remember. All I knew was that...I was different from the other kids. I never fit in because of something that had happened to me. And because I couldn't remember."

A breeze drifted through the garden, chilling Andrea. She wrapped her arms around herself as she gazed at the trickle of water from the fountain. "Last year, after Aunt Clarice died, I decided to move back to Houston. I'm not sure why. It was just something I was...compelled to do.

I got a job teaching in a private school, and then a mutual friend introduced me to Christina Malone. She hired me as Mayela's nanny. The pay was excellent, and I thought it would be nice to live in a real home. I'd never had one...." Andrea trailed off, realizing that maybe she was trying to play on Troy's sympathy after all. A little comfort might not be so bad right now.

She wished he'd put his arms around her and hold her close while she told him the rest of her story. But unfortunately he seemed to have formed an opinion about her already. She hadn't told him the complete truth, and now he didn't trust her. Andrea couldn't blame him, but the distance between them hurt just the same. Especially after last night.

"Go on," Troy prompted

She took a deep breath and released it. "By the time I came to live with the Malones, Christina was already suffering from depression, and Richard was wrapped up in his business. He was rarely home. I knew Mayela needed me, and that made me feel good. Made me feel needed. I was happy for a while, but after Christina's death, I started having dreams...these flashes of memory that were just enough to make me start wondering about my past. I think Christina's death and my bond with Mayela somehow triggered the memories. Mayela was the same age I was when...I lost my father."

"Is that why you started seeing Dr. Bennett?"

Andrea nodded. "She used hypnosis to unleash the memories. I remembered more and more with each session. She's the one who found out where my mother was. That Sunday evening Richard was killed, I remembered something...important. Something I had to see Dr. Bennett about."

"You went to see Dr. Bennett that night?"

Andrea frowned. She'd been going to see Dr. Bennett when she'd left the Perelli home. It had been a matter of urgency. But...why? She couldn't remember. She couldn't even remember if she'd seen Dr. Bennett or not.

"What is it?" Troy asked.

"I don't remember now what I was going to see her about."

"But you do remember seeing her that night?"

Andrea shook her head. "I remember the storm. I remember leaving the house. I remember seeing Mayela. But then...nothing. It's as if everything stopped for me then."

"You remember everything else about your life except for what happened to you that night after you left the Perelli home?"

His tone sounded skeptical. Andrea supposed she could hardly blame him, but it hurt just the same that he didn't believe her.

He paused, then said, "How much of what you've just told me did you remember before you came to my apartment last night?"

"I remembered quite a bit," she admitted softly. "I'd been having these terrible visions...flashes of memory, I guess, but I didn't put it all together until later, until after we...made love."

"That's why you ran out on me?"

She nodded.

He ran a hand through his dark hair. "Damn it, I asked you point-blank last night if there was anything you hadn't told me. I asked you if you were holding out on me. Do you remember?"

Andrea moistened her lips. "I remember."

"You lied to me. You deliberately deceived me."

He turned to her then, his gaze unfathomable. But Andrea knew there were suspicions lurking in those dark depths. She knew there was distrust. She remembered the woman Madison had told her about, the murder suspect who had duped Troy into believing her. He'd been hurt badly by that woman, and now Andrea had done the same thing to him. She wished she could go back and start all over, tell him from the very first about the awful visions and dreams she'd had, and her fears and suspicions about herself. She wished she hadn't been so self-protective.

But it was too late now.

"I didn't tell you because I didn't remember everything," she said desperately. "I was getting all those memories from my past mixed up with what happened to Richard. Everything I remembered…made me look guilty."

"I see." There was an edge to his words that made Andrea flinch. "You used me."

"*No!* At least, not intentionally," she said softly.

He turned to stare at her, and Andrea's heart plummeted at the expression on his face. "Then what would you call it? You knew how I felt about you. You knew if we became involved, if we became lovers, I'd do anything in my power to help you. Are you telling me you didn't count on that all along?"

She shook her head, tears smarting behind her lids. "It wasn't like that."

"But how can I believe you, Andrea? First you tell me you remember nothing, then I find you here with a mother you haven't seen in twenty years. Now you tell me you don't remember what happened the night Richard died, but you remember everything else. Tell me, Andrea. Just what in hell am I suppose to believe?''

She bowed her head. ''I wanted to confide in you from the first. You don't know how badly. But I couldn't. It wasn't just me I had to worry about. I had to think of Mayela. If I'd been arrested, who would have taken care of her?''

''That's another thing,'' he said grimly. ''You were worried about Mayela even before I told you about Richard. You already knew he was dead, didn't you?''

She wanted to deny it, but couldn't. Somehow she *had* known.

''Tell me something, Andrea.''

She looked up at him.

''Were you in love with Richard, or is that one of the things you can't remember?''

''I didn't love him,'' she said quietly. ''I hardly knew him. I agreed to marry him so I would stand a better chance of retaining custody of Mayela when he died.''

''You're saying your marriage was a business arrangement?''

''More or less. Richard was worried that Dorian might challenge my guardianship after he was gone. He thought if we were married, the courts would look more favorably on me.''

''Did he offer you money?''

Andrea wished with all her heart he hadn't had to ask her that question. She wished he would have known her so well, trusted her enough by this time that the answer would have been apparent to him. She closed her eyes against the keen disappointment. ''No,'' she said. ''He didn't offer me money, and I wouldn't have taken it if he had. Mayela was my only concern, and she still is. I love her like a daughter. The ten million dollars Richard left me was a complete surprise. I didn't want anything.''

"What about Paul Bellamy?"

"What about him?"

"Were you in love with him?"

The breeze picked up, drawing another shiver from Andrea as she thought about Paul Bellamy. "I came to hate him," she said. "When I first went to work for Christina and Richard, Paul became…interested in me. I went out with him a couple of times, but when I tried to break it off, he wouldn't leave me alone. His behavior became…obsessive.''

"You have that effect," Troy said, gazing at her.

Something in his eyes made Andrea's heart beat even harder. "You don't believe me. You don't believe anything I've told you. You think I'm lying, don't you?"

"I think your instinct for survival runs pretty damn deep." He scrubbed his face with his hands. "I don't know what to believe anymore."

"Then what are you going to do?" Andrea asked fearfully.

"What I have to do. I'm going to take you back to Houston." He turned to her, his expression grim. "As of this morning, there's a warrant out for your arrest."

"What?" Andrea stared at him in shock. "But I'm innocent!"

He gazed at her as if she were a stranger. "Are you? How can you be so sure of your innocence? I didn't think you could remember what happened the night Richard was killed.''

Andrea tried to swallow past the panic that had risen to her throat. "I can't. Not specifics. But I know I'm not a murderer. I couldn't kill anyone. You have to know that, too, Troy. After last night, you have to know I'm not capable of murder.''

He shook his head. "After last night, I'm not sure of anything. I've risked everything for you, and you're still not even willing to tell me the truth."

"I have told you the truth," Andrea cried. "Please, Troy. You have to believe me. I don't remember what happened that night, but I know I didn't kill Richard. If you take me in, what will happen to Mayela?"

There was no warmth in his expression when he looked at her. Nothing that Andrea could hang on to for comfort when he said, "If I don't take you in, I'm finished. My career is over. But maybe that's what you've wanted all along. A botched investigation. Police misconduct. After last night, you could say I took advantage of you. Seduced you. There's not a jury in the world that would convict you."

She looked at him in despair. "You don't believe that of me. You can't believe it."

"It really doesn't matter what I believe anymore. I'm still a cop. There's a warrant for your arrest, and I have to take you in. I don't have a choice."

Andrea took a deep, shaky breath. A sudden calmness came over her. She knew what she had to do. "All right," she said, standing. "I'll go with you. But first, if it's okay…I'd like to say goodbye to my mother. I may not be able to see her again for a very long time."

TROY STATIONED HIMSELF by the front desk, waiting for Andrea to return. When ten minutes went by, he began to get a little uneasy. He walked down the hall to Julia Evans's room and found Dr. Albrecht coming out.

"Is Andrea still inside with her mother?"

Dr. Albrecht looked at him, perplexed. "Andrea? She left with you half an hour ago."

"But she came back in," Troy said. "She wanted to say goodbye to her mother."

"I've been with Julia ever since the two of you left," Dr. Albrecht told him. "Andrea never came back."

Chapter Sixteen

Andrea was back in Houston before she realized her escape had been just a little too easy. Troy was a seasoned cop. No way she could have gotten away from him unless he'd allowed her to. He'd deliberately given her enough rope to hang herself, and she'd fallen for it. Why would she run if she wasn't guilty?

Andrea groaned inwardly. If Troy hadn't been convinced of her guilt before, he surely was now. Maybe the best thing to do was just to keep going, she thought. She could go somewhere far away, where her past wouldn't matter. She could pretend the memories hadn't come back, that she was just a normal woman, leading a normal life, and maybe someday she might even meet someone else she could fall in love with.

But there would never be anyone like Troy.

She had hurt him deeply by not being honest with him, by not trusting him enough to confide in him, and the only thing she could do now was to honor what little trust he might still have in her by going to the police and turning herself in.

But first there was something she had to do. Someone she had to see. No matter what anyone else thought, Andrea knew deep down she wasn't a murderer. She hadn't killed Richard, and there was only one way to prove it.

She had to remember.

By the time Andrea pulled up in front of Dr. Bennett's house, dusk had fallen. There was a light on upstairs, but the downstairs was completely dark. Andrea wondered if Dr. Bennett had retired for the evening, but it was only a little after seven. Surely she wouldn't mind being disturbed. Not for something this important.

Andrea climbed the porch steps and rang the bell. Several minutes went by before she finally heard footsteps inside, and then Dr. Bennett opened the door and stared at Andrea in surprise.

"I'm sorry to bother you like this," Andrea said. "But I really need to see you, Dr. Bennett. Something's happened."

Dr. Bennett didn't say a word. She drew back the door, and Andrea stepped inside. The foyer was dark, except for a brief trail of light on the stairs. Andrea shivered, suddenly feeling apprehensive. Had she done the right thing by coming here?

As Dr. Bennett led the way to her office, Andrea tried to get her bearings, remembering the other times she'd been in this house. Dr. Bennett's office was at the end of a long hallway. Several rooms opened off the hallway, but the doors were always kept closed. Andrea had no idea what was behind any of them.

Toward the end of the hallway, her steps slowed. A memory tugged at her. Something about this hallway...

"Andrea?"

Dr. Bennett's voice snapped her out of her reverie. Andrea gazed down the hall, where the doctor stood in the doorway of her office, waiting. "Are you all right?"

Andrea nodded. "Yes, I'm fine."

Dr. Bennett motioned her inside the office. "Shall we get started, then?"

Andrea stepped inside the office and looked around. Something was different. "You've changed it," she said. The walls had been painted, and the hardwood floor was covered with carpet.

Dr. Bennett took a seat behind her desk. "I had to. A water pipe broke and flooded this end of the house. Everything had to be replaced."

Andrea glanced around at the pristine surroundings. She could smell the lingering scent of paint, and for some reason, the scent seemed ominous.

"Why are you here, Andrea?" Dr. Bennett asked softly. She picked up a pencil, ready to take notes.

"I've got my memory back."

The pencil snapped in her fingers. "All of it?"

"Most of it," Andrea said. "I remember about…my mother…what she did to my father. I remember seeing…everything through the keyhole in the dark room. You helped me remember."

"The hypnosis helped you to remember," Dr. Bennett said. "When the police told me you were suffering from amnesia again, I was afraid it would be a severe setback. All of our hard work undone. But you say now that you remember…everything?"

Andrea drew a deep breath. "Everything except the night Richard was murdered."

Something flickered in Dr. Bennett's eyes, and she looked down quickly, as if afraid of alarming her patient. "You came here to be hypnotized. Is that it?"

"Yes." Andrea sat forward in her chair. "It's the only way I can prove I didn't do it."

"Are you sure you want to take that risk?"

"What do you mean?"

Dr. Bennett hesitated. "What if the hypnosis doesn't prove your innocence?"

Andrea swallowed. "You think I'm guilty, too, don't you?"

"I didn't say that."

"You didn't have to. But you're wrong, Dr. Bennett. All of you are wrong. I know I'm not capable of murder."

"Your mother was."

"I'm not my mother."

Dr. Bennett smiled faintly. "All right," she said. "We'll try the hypnosis. Do you remember the trigger?"

Andrea nodded. After several sessions, when she had become adept at going under, Dr. Bennett had given Andrea a posthypnotic suggestion that when spoken, automatically triggered a hypnotic trance.

"Why don't you make yourself comfortable on the sofa?"

Andrea did as she was told. Dr. Bennett pulled up a chair and sat down beside her. "Are you feeling relaxed, Andrea?" Her voice was very soothing.

"Starting to."

"Good. Think about the garden outside your bedroom when you were a child. Feel the sunshine on your face? Can you smell the roses?"

"Yes."

"There's a swing in the garden, isn't there, Andrea?"

"Yes."

"It's blowing in the breeze. Back and forth. Back and forth. A gentle motion. So soothing. Back and forth. Back and forth. Do you see it?"

"Yes."

"Is your kitten in the garden with you, Andrea?"

"Yes." She could see him. A white fur ball that had been a present from her father. Andrea cherished him.

"Do you remember his name?"

"Snowflake."

"Pet him, Andrea. Stroke his soft fur."

Andrea grew very still. She slipped into the trance easily. She wasn't asleep. She wasn't dreaming. She was very much aware of Dr. Bennett's benign voice, but everything else drifted away.

"Andrea," Dr. Bennett said, "I want you to go back to Sunday night, two weeks ago. Do you remember?"

"Yes. I'm alone in the house. Dorian and Robert are both out, thank goodness. Mayela's spending the night with a friend, and Richard's already left for the airport. He said there was something he had to do before he caught his plane."

Andrea frowned as she walked through the huge house in her mind. She was all alone, and a storm was brewing outside. She grew frightened, not for herself but for Mayela.

"What are you doing now, Andrea?"

"I'm driving to the Perelli house," Andrea said. "It's raining so hard, I can hardly see, but Mayela will be frightened by the storm. I have to see her."

"You're at the Perelli home. Is Mayela okay?"

"She's fine," Andrea said, skipping ahead in her mind. She was standing in Lauren Perelli's bedroom, and Mayela was hugging Andrea goodbye, clinging a bit when a clap of thunder sounded outside.

"There's somewhere you have to go, isn't there?" Dr. Bennett said softly.

"I have to see you," Andrea said, as, in her mind, she dashed back out into the rain. Earlier, when she was home alone, she'd remembered something her aunt had once said, something about Andrea's mother. Julia had fallen out of a tree as a child and had suffered a severe head injury. They hadn't expected her to live, but somehow she'd pulled through, and it looked as though she'd made a full recovery until some months later when she had a terrible seizure.

The memory was important because, after her sessions with Dr. Bennett, when Andrea had begun remembering her past, she'd been worried that she might have inherited her mother's insanity. Dr. Bennett had even hinted that the predisposition toward violence was often hereditary. But if her mother's problem was caused by an accident, Andrea had nothing to worry about. Still, she'd wanted to talk to Dr. Bennett about this revelation.

"Where are you now, Andrea?"

"At your front door. I'm wondering why you don't answer my ring. The door is ajar, and I can hear voices inside. Loud voices. I think at first that you must be with a patient, and I start to leave, but then, someone starts shouting. A man. I recognize his voice."

The voices were coming from Dr. Bennett's office. Andrea heard Richard shout her name, and thought at first he was calling to her. Then she realized, as she entered the house, that he was shouting to someone about her.

Andrea started down the hallway toward Dr. Bennett's office. She'd never heard Richard so upset. What in the world was he doing here?

Andrea paused outside the door, wondering if she should go in.

"Christina wasn't sick until she came to see you," Richard said in rage. *"You gave her those pills to make her depressed, and then you gave her an overdose of amphetamines, so that with her history of depression, the*

police wouldn't look twice at the cause of death. You killed her!''

''That's a lie,'' Dr. Bennett said. ''You'll never be able to prove it.''

''Won't I?'' There was silence, then he said, ''I found these in your room, Dorian. I've had the contents analyzed. They're depressants. What were you doing—slipping them into Christina's food every time you came to visit her? She was always so much worse after you left. I've always known you were a cold, greedy bitch, but I never thought you capable of murder. I hope you rot in prison.''

Andrea's hand was on the knob. She started to open the door, but before she could, three shots rang out in rapid succession. Bang! Bang! Bang!

Andrea jerked open the door, startled to find Richard facing her. He was clutching his chest. Blood oozed between his fingers, and for a moment, their eyes met and clung. Then he fell forward into her arms.

His weight drove them back against the wall. Andrea fell hard, trapped for a moment by Richard's inert body. She struggled from under him just as Dorian appeared in the doorway. She stared down at Andrea and lifted the gun.

''Don't kill her,'' Dr. Bennett said behind her. ''She's our scapegoat.''

Andrea tried to scramble away from them. Her hands and clothes were covered in blood. Richard's blood.

Dr. Bennett grabbed her arm. Andrea fought her, but the woman was stronger than she looked. She said to Dorian, ''Help me hold her down.''

Dorian did as she was told, taking pleasure in twisting Andrea's arm painfully behind her. Dr. Bennett reached for her medical bag. She extracted a syringe, Andrea screamed and struggled harder.

"What is that?" Dorian asked.

"Just a mild sedative. Something to make her more susceptible to hypnotic suggestion. I'll inject it between her fingers, so the needle mark can't be detected. In a few hours, the drug won't even show up in her bloodstream and she won't remember a thing."

Andrea felt the jab of the needle between her fingers, and almost immediately, her body grew limp. She fought the effects of the drug, but to no avail. Dr. Bennett's soothing voice was taking her deeper and deeper into the trance.

IT WAS NEARLY eight o'clock, and Andrea was nowhere to be found. Troy sat at his desk at the station, brooding about the day's events. Should he have brought Andrea in himself? Had he been wrong in giving her one last chance to do the right thing?

Whether he'd been wrong or not was beside the point now. He had to figure out what to do next. If Andrea had decided to run—and it looked more and more as if she had—he'd have to go after her. When a person ran, it was usually because he or she was guilty, and Troy would be damned before he'd let a murderer go free.

Even one he'd fallen in love with.

He rubbed his eyes wearily, wishing to hell he'd decided to become anything but a cop.

His phone rang and he picked it up, hoping it was Andrea. "Stoner."

"Troy? It's Leanne. Listen. I just got something in I think you need to see." She paused, then said, "It could blow your case wide open."

"I'm on my way down." Troy hung up the phone and took off at a run.

Leanne was waiting for him. "Take a look at this."

"What is it?"

"It's a photocopy of Dr. Claudia Bennett's yearbook picture."

Troy stared down at the image on the paper. The woman, though years younger, looked nothing like the Claudia Bennett he knew. The discrepancies were so pronounced that not even age could have wrought such a change.

"That's not the woman who came in here claiming to be Dr. Bennett," Leanne said. "I got a good look at her that day. There's no way. And something else. You know that story you told me about Dr. Bennett's agoraphobia and about the housekeeper who died in the fire?"

"She called her Marlena."

Leanne nodded. "I had the police report on the fire faxed to me. The woman's name was Marlena Andersen, except…there's one small problem. Marlena Andersen died five years *before* the fire."

Troy stared at her. "Wait a minute. Are you saying Bennett's housekeeper was using a fake identity?"

"Looks that way. You know who I'm betting that housekeeper was, don't you?"

"The woman we know as Claudia Bennett."

"Exactly. She took Marlena Andersen's identity, and then when Claudia Bennett died, she took her identity."

"And her profession," Troy said. "She's been practicing psychiatry all these years."

"The inmates are in charge of the asylum," Leanne said dryly. "How would you like to be relying on her for your mental well-being?"

Troy remembered Andrea's words earlier. *She used*

*hypnosis to unleash the memories. I remembered more
and more with each session. She's the one who found out
where my mother was.*

Suddenly he knew why Andrea hadn't turned herself
in yet. He knew where she would have gone to for help
in restoring the rest of her memory.

He jumped up and headed for the door.

"SHE'S REMEMBERED everything," Dorian said in disgust. "I thought you said you could take care of her
memory. You said that the night you went to see her in
the hospital. You didn't do it then," Dorian complained.

"I didn't expect Stoner to come back to her room. But
I'll take care of it now," Dr. Bennett promised.

Andrea had come out of her trance just seconds ago to
find her wrists bound behind her and Dorian holding a
gun on her.

"Who are you?" Andrea said to Dr. Bennett.

Dr. Bennett was busy filling a syringe, so Dorian answered for her. "Her name is Helena Kouriakis. She's
my sister."

Sister! Of course! Andrea couldn't understand why she
hadn't seen the resemblance before. Maybe because Dr.
Bennett, who was really Helena Kouriakis, tried so hard
to disguise her appearance. The blue contacts, which
were gone now, and the unnatural white makeup that
covered her olive complexion.

Andrea glared up at Dorian in disgust. "You killed
your own daughter," she said.

"Stepdaughter," Dorian clarified, as if the distinction
made all the difference in the world. But Andrea knew
that even if Christina had been Dorian's own flesh and
blood, she would have stopped at nothing to get what she
wanted. The money. Always the money.

"I've never known anyone so evil."

"Try your own mother," Dorian said slyly. "She stabbed your father right in front of you. That's why you're so crazy."

"I'm not crazy." Andrea tried to keep her voice even as she struggled furiously with the bindings at her wrists.

"Sure, you are. Everyone thinks so. Even the police. Even your Sergeant Stoner," Dorian added maliciously.

Andrea flinched inwardly. Dorian's words struck home. Troy might not think her crazy, but he certainly had his doubts about her. By now, he probably thought she'd skipped town.

"You brought this on yourself," Dorian said hatefully. "Richard was mine. I waited so long for him. After Christina died, he should have married me. And he would have, too, if you hadn't gone to him with your lies about me."

"They weren't lies," Andrea said. "I knew you didn't love Mayela. You only wanted the money."

"And so you convinced Richard to marry you and give *you* custody of Mayela. You're very clever," Dorian said with grudging admiration. "I'll give you that."

"He would have thrown you out a long time ago," Andrea said. The bindings had loosened, and she worked to free one of her hands. "Only, he suspected you were conspiring with Paul Bellamy. He didn't want to tip his hand before he had the proof he needed to go to the police."

"Bellamy's a fool," Dorian said. "Why would I waste my time with the likes of him?"

"The broken skylight," Andrea said. "Was that meant for me or Mayela?"

Dorian shrugged. "I knew the storm would terrify her. I knew she would call out for you as she always did. I just wasn't sure which of you would come running across the bridge first. Either scenario had possibilities. With Mayela out of the way and you in prison for murder, who else would have inherited Richard's estate? Robert? I don't think so. He would have gambled the fortune away in a matter of months. And if you had died under all that glass, an unfortunate accident as it were, I would have become Mayela's guardian, controlling all her money. Just as I once did Christina's.''

They'd thought of everything, Andrea thought. Even going so far as to plant seeds of doubt in her own mind.

"You were up on the roof when the glass fell," Andrea said. "I saw you."

"Not me," Dorian said. "You saw my sister. She's always been very adept at creating...accidents."

Helena turned with the syringe. The needle gleamed in the light.

"What are you going to do?" Andrea asked weakly. Her hands were almost free. A surge of adrenaline shot through her, but she had to remain calm. She had to wait for her chance because Dorian still held a gun on her.

"I'm going to do the same thing I tried to do that night Sergeant Stoner caught me outside your hospital room," Helena said. "I'm going to make sure it's a long, long time before you get your memory back this time. And when you do, Dorian and I will have fixed it so that no one will believe you. They'll think you're insane, just like your dear mother. Maybe they'll even give you a room next to hers."

Andrea pretended to be so frightened she could hardly move. But as Helena bent down to administer the drug, Andrea's hand shot out and grabbed her. She twisted Helena's wrist until the needle fell from her fingers.

Andrea rolled from the sofa, still clutching Helena's

arm. The two of them struggled for what seemed like an eternity. The woman was older than Andrea by at least twenty years, but she also outweighed Andrea by that much and she was strong. She shoved Andrea away from her, and Andrea stumbled, falling heavily against the desk.

Helena was on her before Andrea could catch her balance. The older woman bent Andrea back against the desk as her hands encircled Andrea's throat. Stars exploded behind Andrea's lids. She flailed her arms, trying to find a weapon. Her lungs threatening to explode, Andrea wrapped her hand around the base of a lamp and brought it up as hard as she could against the side of Helena's skull.

For a split second, the woman's hands remained around Andrea's throat. Then she slid to the floor without a sound. Blood gushed from the gash in her temple as she lay motionless at Andrea's feet.

Andrea struggled for breath. Dorian stared down at her sister in disbelief. Then she raised the gun and leveled it at Andrea.

"You really lost it this time, Andrea. You attacked your own psychiatrist. Imagine how the headlines will read in the morning."

Andrea was still clutching the lamp, but Dorian didn't seem to notice. "She's your sister," Andrea said. "Don't you even care whether she's alive or dead?"

"Of course I care," Dorian said. "My sister has always been the one person in my life I could count on. Ever since we were little girls, she always wanted to please me. Take care of me. She'd do anything for me. But I have to think of myself now. And Mayela, of course. The poor child needs me. With you in prison, or in a psychiatric hospital, there's no one standing in my way. I'll finally have what I've worked so hard for all these years.''

"Richard's money," Andrea said, and with that, she hurled the lamp across the room as hard as she could. It missed Dorian by inches, but it was enough to catch her off guard. Andrea flung herself across the room toward her. The gun went off, and Andrea felt the dull punch of the bullet in her shoulder. The force flung her backward. Andrea stumbled, tried to catch her balance, but couldn't. The room spun around her. She dropped to her knees, clutching her shoulder.

Dorian lifted the gun again. This time she aimed for Andrea's face. Andrea squeezed her eyes closed, wondering fleetingly if the next bullet would hurt more or less than the first.

Then, as if in a dream, she heard Troy's voice order Dorian to drop the gun. A woman's voice began reading Dorian her rights. Andrea didn't remember lying down on the floor, but when she opened her eyes, she was flat on her back and Troy was gazing down at her with so much tenderness, Andrea wanted to cry.

"I didn't kill Richard," she said.

"I know. You can tell me the whole story later. Right now you need to save your strength. We've got an ambulance on the way."

"I'm not crazy," she said.

"I am," he said. "Crazy about you."

Her heart fluttered with hope. "Then...you forgive me for not telling you about my memories? For running away from you?"

He cleared his throat gruffly. "Right now I'd forgive you just about anything. Only..."

"What?"

He squeezed her hand. "Hang in there, okay?"

She squeezed his hand back. "I'm crazy about you, too."

Epilogue

Six months later…

She wore white, a dress so pristine it dazzled her eyes as she gazed at her reflection in the mirror. Andrea couldn't believe this day had finally arrived, that in just a few moments, she would be married, truly married, to the man she loved more than life itself. Soon she and Troy and Mayela would be starting a whole new life together. A wonderful life, in spite of the darkness.

It hadn't been easy, coping with the memories of her past, or thinking about the mind control Dr. Bennett had practiced on her. The evil plot she and Dorian had concocted had very nearly destroyed them all. Both Richard and Christina had been the victims of the sisters' greed, but thank God Mayela had been spared. Thank God, as well, that she seemed to be suffering no long-term effects, as Andrea had.

Andrea would always be grateful to Madison for the way she'd taken care of the little girl while Andrea had been in the hospital, recovering from the bullet wound. Because of Madison, Mayela had a chance to resume a normal childhood, and because of Troy, they both had a chance to love again.

Someone knocked on the door of the changing room, and Andrea turned from the mirror. "Come in."

Madison opened the door and stuck her head in. She wore a long flowing dress in dark red velvet, befitting the Christmas season. "It's time," she said. "Are you ready?"

Andrea smiled. "You have no idea how ready I am."

"Then let's go."

Troy's father, Earl, who would be giving her away, waited outside for her. The church took Andrea's breath away, decorated with hundreds of white and red roses and tiny white lights that glittered like diamonds in the candlelight. Everything was perfect, almost too beautiful to be real. Andrea thought for a moment she must be dreaming, but if she was, it was a dream like no other, and she didn't ever want to wake up.

She took Earl's arm, and together they paused while Mayela, looking adorable in a red velvet dress trimmed with white lace, scattered rose petals in her wake. She was followed by Madison, and then, almost too quickly, it was time for Andrea to walk down the aisle.

She grew nervous and almost stumbled, but Troy's father held her steady. And then she saw Troy, looking so handsome in his black tuxedo, waiting for her at the altar. He smiled, and everything calmed inside Andrea.

With strong, steady steps, she started down the aisle toward him. Toward their future. And she knew if she lived to be a hundred, she would never forget a moment of this perfect, perfect day.

EVER HAD ONE OF THOSE DAYS?

TO DO:

☑ at the supermarket buying two dozen muffins that your son just remembered to tell you he needed for the school treat, you realize you left your wallet at home

☑ at work just as you're going into the big meeting, you discover your son took your presentation to school, and you have his hand-drawn superhero comic book

☑ your mother-in-law calls to say she's coming for a month-long visit

☑ finally at the end of a long and exasperating day, you escape from it all with an entertaining, humorous and always romantic Love & Laughter book!

ENJOY
LOVE & LAUGHTER™
EVERY DAY!

For a preview, turn the page....

*Here's a sneak peek at
Carrie Alexander's THE AMOROUS HEIRESS
Available September 1997...*

———————

"YOU'RE A VERY popular lady," Jed Kelley observed as Augustina closed the door on her suitors.

She waved a hand. "Just two of a dozen." Technically true since her grandmother had put her on the open market. "You're not afraid of a little competition, are you?"

"Competition?" He looked puzzled. "I thought the position was mine."

Augustina shook her head, smiling coyly. "You didn't think Grandmother was the final arbiter of the decision, did you? I say a trial period is in order." No matter that Jed Kelley had miraculously passed Grandmother's muster, Augustina felt the need for a little propriety. But, on the other hand, she could be married before the summer was out and be free as a bird, with the added bonus of a husband it wouldn't be all that difficult to learn to love.

She got up the courage to reach for his hand, and then just like that, she—Miss Gussy Gutless Fairchild—was holding Jed Kelley's hand. He looked down at their linked hands. "Of course, you don't really know what sort of work I can do, do you?"

A funny way to put it, she thought absently, cradling his callused hand between both of her own. "We can get to know each other, and then, if that works out..." she murmured. *Wow.* If she'd known what this arranged marriage thing was all about, she'd have been a supporter of Grandmother's campaign from the start!

"Are you a palm reader?" Jed asked gruffly. His voice was as raspy as sandpaper and it was rubbing her all the right ways, but the question flustered her. She dropped his hand.

"I'm sorry."

"No problem," he said, "as long as I'm hired."

"Hired!" she scoffed. "What a way of putting it!"

Jed folded his arms across his chest. "So we're back to the trial period."

"Yes." Augustina frowned and her gaze dropped to his work boots. Okay, so he wasn't as well off as the majority of her suitors, but really, did he think she was going to *pay* him to marry her?

"Fine, then." He flipped her a wave and, speechless, she watched him leave. She was trembling all over like a malaria victim in a snowstorm, shot with hot charges and cold shivers until her brain was numb. This couldn't be true. Fantasy men didn't happen to nice girls like her.

"Augustina?"

Her grandmother's voice intruded on Gussy's privacy. "Ahh. There you are. I see you met the new gardener?"

 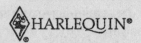

HARLEQUIN WOMEN KNOW ROMANCE WHEN THEY SEE IT.

And they'll see it on **ROMANCE CLASSICS**, the new 24-hour TV channel devoted to romantic movies and original programs like the special **Harlequin® Showcase of Authors & Stories.**

The **Harlequin® Showcase of Authors & Stories** introduces you to many of your favorite romance authors in a program developed exclusively for Harlequin® readers.

Watch for the **Harlequin® Showcase of Authors & Stories** series beginning in the summer of 1997.

If you're not receiving ROMANCE CLASSICS, call your local cable operator or satellite provider and ask for it today!

Escape to the network of your dreams.

ROMANCE CLASSICS

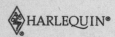